MW00533828

RACE
for
JUSTICE

Book Three
of the
Run for Your Life
Adventure
Trilogy

Pamela Beason

This is a work of fiction. Names, characters, places, and incidents are products of the author's imagination or are used fictitiously and are not to be construed as real. Although Bellingham, Washington is a real place, the Quarrel Tayson Laboratories and other companies were invented for the sake of the story. Any semblance to actual events, locales, organizations, or persons, living or dead, is entirely coincidental.

WILDWING PRESS
3301 Brandywine Court
Bellingham, Washington 98226

Copyright © 2018 Pamela Beason
ISBN-10: 0-9976420-8-4
ISBN-13: 978-0-9976420-8-7
www.pamelabeason.com

Cover design by Christine Savoie

All rights reserved. No part of this book may be used or reproduced in any manner whatsoever without written permission, except in the case of brief quotations embodied in articles and reviews.

Prologue

Just when I thought the mysterious P.A. Patterson was gone for good, my sponsors at Dark Horse Networks forward a message from him to me. It's an invitation to a multi-day endurance race that is being held for the very first time.

Extreme Africa Endurance Challenge – Zimbabwe

An exciting 500-kilometer race that crosses rivers, canyons, and winds through hills, forests, and grasslands. All efforts will be made to keep racers safe, but wild animals such as elephants, hippos, lions, and leopards may be encountered.

Not to mention bandits and thugs who may lie in wait along the way. I've always wanted to participate in a race in Africa, and Zimbabwe is my mother's birthplace. But when I was growing up and my parents were still alive, they told me tales of such violence there that I'm reluctant to visit that country without an armed escort.

Brand new races are often disasters, with a lack of decent food or comfortable sleeping accommodations. I agree with my sponsors at Dark Horse Networks that it's generally best to avoid them until the second or third year, after the kinks have been worked out. But this time, Clark and Kent Nilsen seem eager for me to participate. *Africa is a huge untapped market for our services*, they write.

I owe the Nilsen brothers, big time. They helped me set up a company to buy my property at WildRun, and they installed my security gate there. They monitor my fan mail and screen out most of the malicious messages. Without their financial sponsorship, I wouldn't be able to race at all.

The email message includes a link to a website. When I click and go there, I am bombarded with advertising about wonderful accommodations for racers and media and fans— exotic game lodges and luxury hotels. There's even a video. I click the play button and watch a trio of lean dark-skinned runners lope along an exotic course. Zebras graze in the distance. As the runners pass a checkpoint, the camera zooms in on the smiles of enthusiastic fans clustered together behind a barrier tape. Among them is a woman photographer with curly chestnut hair pulled up into a ponytail. With her eye pressed to a camera, she turns with the crowd, tracking the racers. The crowd then disperses, leaving the photographer, who lowers her camera and looks directly at whoever is filming this vid. It feels like she's staring into my eyes.

My heart stops. My whole body throbs with a sudden longing to throw myself into that woman's arms. I play the vid over and over again, stopping it every few frames to stare at her straight nose, her curly brown hair. When she looks up, she's smiling, just a little with her lips closed, like my mother did when she had a secret.

Could it be? I found my brother last year, after four years of believing he was most likely murdered along with my mom and dad.

I saw my parents' bodies lying in a pool of blood on our living room floor. Could it be possible that my mother didn't die that night? Could she really be alive?

The woman turns away, following the crowd, and I'm not sure. Her hair is longer and several shades lighter than my mother's. She's wearing a khaki uniform that implies she's working there.

Mom?

I know it's too much to hope for. Maybe I no longer remember what Mom looked like. The only picture I have is small and grainy, a photo of her with her colleagues at work.

Videos can be altered. If my enemies suspect I'm Amelia Robinson, then they know I have a personal connection to Africa. This P.A. Patterson could be luring me to Zimbabwe, where I'll be eaten by a lion or ambushed by armed thugs, and die an easily explained death. This might be a setup by the black-clad ninja invaders I escaped from four years ago.

I know this might be a trap designed especially for me.

But I also know that my next race will be in Zimbabwe.

One

Seven months later

The two-story red brick building no longer looks like a scientific laboratory. Most of its windows have been broken. Only a few sharp teeth of dusty glass remain in the rusted metal frames, making the openings appear vaguely carnivorous. The vegetation on the flat roof is so thick that I can see tall grass waving in the slight breeze and vines dangling over the exterior walls. Various items of clothing dangle from the windows; a striped skirt and a dish towel flapping from the second floor, two tattered T-shirts from the lower, a pair of tiny child's underpants threatening to take flight from the corner window.

People in town keep saying that now since The Leader is gone and a new guy is president, they have hope for the future. Nothing in front of me looks much like hope, unless you count the rows of plants in the garden at the side of the building. I guess planting a seed implies a certain amount of optimism, doesn't it?

In the lumpy dirt yard, a group of ragged kids kick a lopsided soccer ball that sorely needs more air. When the ball flies my way, I side-step and watch it smack into the sagging, bullet-pocked sign beside me, which rattles on its rusting metal feet as the ball drops to the ground below. The sun has nearly faded the letters away, but if you look really close, you can still make out the words VF Research Laboratory. For some reason, I expected to it to be Quarrel Tayson Laboratory, the name of the giant pharmaceutical corporation my mom used to work for, but no, the ancient guy at the hotel said this was the only research lab in town. *Was* being the operative word.

I kick the ball back toward the kids, making an unladylike yelp as my foot connects because the action is surprisingly painful, given that I'm wearing sandals, and the ball is now flatter than ever. The kids giggle and gape at me, their gaze scouring every inch of my body. Their shorts and tees are more holes than cloth. Squatters. At least I hope they're squatters. Nobody should have to pay to live in this ruin of a building near the center of Victoria Falls.

This, I'm learning, is modern Zimbabwe, even in the middle of the 21st century. Although people are no longer getting slaughtered all over the place, I guess it's still the country that my mother fled from. That's what a corrupt leader can do to an entire nation. It's depressing. We've had shady politicians in the United States, but so far Americans have never allowed the government to drag us down to this level.

I know the former dictator ruled Zimbabwe for nearly half a century, becoming more ruthless and more violent as time wore on. Ten months ago he finally dropped off the political map, but still, nobody will even mention his name. They just call him The Leader. Even though he's not, anymore.

I arrived a day early so I could check out the area. Before I was born, my mother started her career as a biochemist here. That was when she was Amy Jansen, before she married my American father and became Amy Robinson. I'd hoped to talk to someone at this laboratory about her, and ask about P.A. Patterson, too. Maybe show someone those curious spreadsheets my father saved, see if someone from the company can explain the importance of the codes and dates. I can't ask those questions at the Quarrel Tayson headquarters in my old home town because it would be too easy for them to guess where I got those files. Then they could also guess who I really am, when I've managed to stay hidden all these years.

Apparently, my plan to start at Mom's old laboratory was lame. Clearly, I will glean no information here about any employee from the past or present. Now I really have no clue about how to find my Mom Lookalike, or any of her family.

I could kick myself. I didn't think my African relatives would be waiting at the airport to greet me, but I thought I'd be able to locate them easily enough once I got to Zimbabwe.

I'm sort of glad Mom's not around to see these ruins.

Or is she?

I can't get that vid out of my head. It makes no sense that my mother and father would fake their deaths and leave me on my own at fourteen. If it all turns out to be an elaborate hoax, could I forgive my parents? Would I still love them if I found out everything they ever told me was a lie?

I shake my head to clear those cobwebs of doubt from my brain. Surely no parent would ever be that cruel. But not knowing for sure is making me crazy.

These brief trips down Insanity Lane give me a small glimpse of what life must be like for my brother Aaron, who has problems sorting out reality from fiction. At least I know what I've seen—my parents' bodies on the living room floor, the masked ninjas coming after me, the woman on this new vid who looks so much like Mom. Those fragmented images are all real, even if the pieces don't fit into a coherent whole.

Aaron, on the other hand, spent years imprisoned and drugged out of his gourd for a fictional mental illness, while being brainwashed into thinking he was Jaime Ramirez and that his memories were psychotic delusions. The only living being Aaron truly trusts is Bailey.

There's no denying that Bailey is real, as improbable as an elephant in your back yard might seem.

I study with free online sites whenever I can, trying to keep up with my friends who are lucky enough to afford college. My vocabulary lesson for today from my Wordage app was *enigma—something that is confusing or difficult to understand.* That's been my life for the last four years: an enigma.

Geographastic, the other educational app I use a lot, seems to know I'm in Africa, because this morning it informed me that Akanda National Park is on the coast of Gabon, which, to my surprise, turns out to be another country in Africa, but on the west side of the continent. There's a Gabon viper in the zoo where I work, but I never thought much about its name. I don't even stick my head into the snake house if I can avoid it. Give me a mammal any day of the week. And then that thought reminds me that I should call my housemate, Sabrina Vasile, to see how she's getting along with Bailey and our goats.

As if it knows I'm thinking about it, my cell buzzes against my hip. When I put my hand into my pocket, one of the older African boys turns to stare in my direction. His black eyes have the burning focus of a hunter. His gaze traces my arm down to my pocket. I slowly extract my hand and force myself to smile and wave before I turn and walk away. I recognize a predator when I see one. I saw a lot of them when I was alone on the streets after I lost my parents. My cell phone is a cheap model, but it's probably worth more than anything his family owns. Before I pull the phone from my pocket, I make sure that I am out of sight and even glance over my shoulder to be sure Black Eyes hasn't followed me. And the desk clerk at the hotel last night warned me to be watchful for robberies and other violent acts in town.

I've made up my mind not to think about what "other violent acts" might include. My imagination is already expert at conjuring up scenes of blood and suffering. However, so far everything promised in the race invitation seems legit, and as near as I can tell, nobody is following me, so I'm not quite as paranoid as I was when I stepped off the plane yesterday.

RACE CAMP - ONE HOUR, my calendar app reminds me. I'm going to be late if I don't hustle, but I tell myself to stride quickly and purposefully. Running could get me mistaken for prey. This morning, I dressed as simply as I could in a khaki skirt and blue T-shirt and sandals so I wouldn't be a tempting robbery target.

I pass the guarded gates that block off the park surrounding Victoria Falls—not the town, but the actual waterfall. I spent a smidgeon of my own money to take a tour this morning, and frankly, I was a little disappointed. Victoria Falls is supposed to be one of the seven natural wonders of the world, and sure, the Zambezi River drops hundreds of feet here and the falls are wide, but you can't stand in one place and be wowed. The falls cascade into a big crack in the earth. From most of the viewpoints, you have to stare at that water sideways and you can't even see much because of all the mist that billows out of the canyon below.

The best way to experience Victoria Falls, I heard the guide say, is to sign up for an uber-expensive helicopter tour. I don't think my sponsors would foot the bill for that, and a twenty-minute ride that costs hundreds of dollars is not something a lowly Habitat Maintenance Technician like me can afford. After feeding all the creatures that depend on me at home, I'm lucky to scrape together enough to treat myself to a hot fudge sundae at the Dairy Queen.

Returning to the small hotel where I stayed last night, I retrieve my duffel from the nice woman at the front desk, tipping her two American dollars for keeping it safe. Then it's only a couple of short blocks to the race camp, which is good because the toes of my right foot are still smarting from kicking that plastic soccer pancake.

The camp is not much to look at, just a collection of low buildings surrounded by a stone-and-cement wall topped with broken glass. I show the guard at the gate my passport and he checks me in.

"Room eight." He points to one of the low buildings. "We will dress for dinner tonight, Miss." Checking his watch, he warns, "But you are to wear your race uniform to the opening ceremony in one hour, in the mess hall." He points to a huge pole frame building with a tin roof, which already is crowded with people.

Room eight turns out to be a pretty basic accommodation, but it's only for a couple of nights. The room holds two narrow beds, each with a couple of towels stacked on top of their rainbow-colored bedspreads. Two lockers, one table and chair. Whoever my roommate is, she's not here yet. I stash my gear in one of the lockers.

We will dress for dinner tonight, Miss. Uh-huh. I didn't come prepared with formal wear. I don't even *own* formal wear. I pull out the only item I brought that might look slightly better than what I've got on. My slinky emerald green sundress slithers back into its former shape no matter how I wad it up inside my suitcase. I drape the dress across one of the beds to claim my sleeping space. Then I trot to the women's room, where I do my best to rinse off the worst grime in one of the three showers before I pull on my race uniform, a gold jersey with the galloping stallion logo of my sponsors, Dark Horse Networks, and my black running tights. We've been warned about thorny brush and snakes, so there's no way I'm wearing shorts out there, no matter how hot it is.

"Contestants to the mess hall, contestants to the mess hall," a loudspeaker screeches outside. I shove my feet into my running shoes, and stride quickly and purposefully to the pole building.

Under that metal roof, it's loud and crowded, with racers and their families and support teams excitedly milling around long tables. I'm a team of one so far, which feels a little lonely, but at least I don't take up a lot of room or make much noise.

A chubby emcee with a microphone stands on the far side, centering himself in a rather weird giant horseshoe arrangement made of flowers and vines. At the top of the horseshoe is a yellow and black banner that reads *Extreme Africa Endurance Challenge.* In front of him are two long tables with huge bouquets of flowers and signs that say RESERVED.

After an ear-splitting screech of electronic feedback that gets everyone's attention, the emcee asks us all to sit down. There are far more people in here than chairs, so his request ends up inciting a musical-chairs grabfest with only the fastest folks winning seats. The rest of us shuffle like stray cattle to the far side of the building.

Then the introductions begin. Dignitaries and sponsors dressed in everything from military uniforms to tuxedos peel off from the crowd to join the emcee. Since Zimbabwe has more than a dozen national languages and most of the competitors are African, each introduction is stated in English, then repeated in several languages that are incomprehensible to me. I spend my time surveying the crowd, looking for white women with chestnut hair. Only a few white folks are present, so it doesn't take long to see that none of the women look anything like my mother.

I also search the white faces for my teammate, X, short for

Xavier Jones. Ten months ago I competed with X and his older brother Jason in the Ski to Sea relay race in Bellingham, Washington, where I lived until my parents were murdered. Jason, with his collection of specialized artificial feet, ended up stealing the limelight as the gimp hero of the event, but it was X who started our team off in a lead position. I want him to have this chance to shine on his own, so I invited him to be my partner. Besides, Jason is so busy right now appearing on talk shows and cereal boxes that he doesn't have time to romp around Africa with me.

I don't see Xavier's sand-colored hair and freckled face anywhere. When the emcee tells us introductions of racers will begin, my stomach begins to churn out acid. Pointing to the floral hoop over his head, the emcee explains that as the names are called, racers will enter through the horseshoe and take their place at the reserved tables up front. Making a shooing motion with both hands, he instructs the competitors to go outside and wait to hear their names called.

This seems incredibly hokey, but whatever. The racers dribble out the sides of the building and walk around to the back of the emcee and the horseshoe gate as the translations echo over the speakers. We competitors scrutinize each other. Each team has one female, one male. Both have to make it to the finish line to score.

There are three pale-skinned racers in our group. Two are speaking German to each other. The other tall freckled white girl is chatting with a dark-skinned dude. Their English sounds vaguely Australian to me, and I only pick up about every third word.

Where the hell is *my* pale-skinned partner? A touch on my arm makes me whirl around. Instead of finding X, I am greeted by Marco Senai, a perpetually emaciated and incredibly talented runner from Kenya.

Marco grins broadly, showing his straight white teeth. He holds out a hand. "I am honored to race you again."

I put my hand in his long slender fingers. "I'm glad to see you, too, Marco."

Marco Senai has the most wonderful, musical accent. Even his laugh sounds melodious as he chuckles and adds, "This time, Marco Senai will triumph over Tanzania Grey."

Tanzania Grey. That's the name I gave myself when I reinvented my life. To further disguise that Amelia Robinson girl I used to be, I twisted my history, telling everyone my black father came from Tanzania, when in reality it is my white mother, Amy Robinson, who grew up in Zimbabwe. My dad is an accountant from Chicago.

Was from Zimbabwe, *was* from Chicago. Sometimes even I get confused with all the fictional biography details I created for myself. But it's important to keep up the lies, because the ninjas who killed my parents and made a psycho zombie out of my brother are probably still on my trail.

On my left, a slender young woman eyes me. She's a walking piece of sculpture with flawless blue-black skin. "What tribe are you?" she asks.

I've been in Africa for less than two days, and I'm already sick of that question. "American."

"Ah." She says something in another language to the man beside her, who takes a quick glance at me, nods and repeats,

"Ah." Then they both turn away, dismissing me.

I thought that with my caramel-colored skin and black hair, I'd fit right in here. But apparently, being tribeless, I'm a worthless mongrel.

I notice that nobody asks the Germans what tribe *they're* from.

The introductions begin with Team One, a pair of Zimbabwean runners who receive roaring cheers from the audience. After that, as names are called, competitors peel off from our cluster to stroll through the flower horseshoe to much more subdued applause from the audience. As our numbers dwindle, I start to panic.

"Team Seven. Gretchen Vogel!"

The tall white girl separates from the flock and dashes through the horseshoe. She is welcomed by only a few polite clapping sounds. When her husband or brother, Walter Vogel, answers the call, he gets even less response. I'm not the only racer here with no groupies.

No X. Was his flight delayed or something? Will I be disqualified if he doesn't show up for this introduction?

"Team Eight," the emcee's voice booms over the loudspeaker. "Tanzania Grey!"

He pronounces it in the British fashion, tan-*zane*-ee-ah. I hope that nobody will start calling me Zany again. I hate that stupid name; I call myself Tana.

I force a smile onto my face and stroll through the stupid horseshoe blossoms, waving to the crowd with one hand like the Queen of England. There are only a few polite claps. I have no family or friends here, only a few fans who know my name.

A gorgeous muscular young man clad in a leopard-skin loincloth and matching armbands hands me a race bib, and then a photographer steps in front of me and an old-fashioned flash goes off right in my face. I'm blinded for a few seconds and have to awkwardly grope my way toward the table as the emcee stutters, "And...and...for Team Eight..."

Xavier Jones has stood me up.

I contemplate sliding out of sight under the tablecloth.

My quest to find my Zimbabwean roots is going to be over before it even begins.

Two

"**S**ebastian Callendro!"

My mouth drops open. I twist in my seat to watch my friend Bash trot through the flowers. The crowd cheers. People the world over still know his name, even though his father, President T.L. Garrison, has been out of the White House for months now.

Bash accepts his race bib from Mr. Loincloth, and then pulls out the chair beside me and slides into it. Last time I saw him, The President's Secret Love Child was hiding out in a small village in New Mexico and dressing like a *narcotraficante*. Now Sebastian Callendro has shaved his bandito mustache and goatee and he's letting his dark brown hair grow long again.

Grinning, he plucks an orange flower from the table decoration in front of him, jabs the stem into my hair behind my left ear, and then grabs my fingers and holds up our joined hands for the crowd, shouting, "Team Eight!"

Two more flashes stab my eyes. Through fake-smile lips, I murmur, "W-T-F, Bash?"

He responds, "W-N."

"What the heck does *that* mean?"

He grins even wider. "Why not?"

"I was expecting Xavier Jones."

"I made him an offer he couldn't refuse."

Bash may not welcome the media attention he received after his relationship to the U.S. President became public knowledge, but he's not above taking advantage of Bio-Pop's wealth when he wants to. He paid to rescue my brother Aaron and transport him across the country, and he pays for Aaron's private school. For all I know, Bash may have given Xavier, a freshman in college, tuition money for years to come.

"I told you why I was coming," I remind him.

Bash and my housemate Sabrina are the only people who know the whole sad story of Amelia Robinson. Although this P.A. Patterson who sent the invitation knows things about my family that only a friend or the killers could, so maybe I should add him to that list.

While I'm happy to see Sebastian Callendro, I'm not sure I want him as my race partner. As The President's Son, Bash tends to attract the kind of attention I don't need. Paparazzi who want to take his photo. Kidnappers planning ransom or extortion. Terrorists who want to behead him to make a political statement.

On the other hand, I'm not exactly the safest person to hang out with, either. I could meet up with a convenient "accident" at any time.

If I, a lowly zoo cage cleaner, die here, it won't exactly rip a hole in the fabric of the universe. Sebastian Callendro, however, has brilliant ideas that could make the world a better place, and the talent to make them into reality. Plus, I personally would never forgive myself if he died on my watch. "It's too dangerous, Bash."

"Then you shouldn't be here, either."

That's Sebastian Callendro for you. There's no way to out-argue him.

"The distance of the race has now been set at 350 kilometers, and the race has been shortened to four days," the host states. "The government of Zimbabwe will host all the competitors for the fifth day here at our luxurious race camp, giving them more time to explore our beautiful country."

Bash and I exchange mystified looks. The original race information said five hundred kilometers and five days. A buzz moves up the table as the racers react to the change, but nobody seems to mind that the course is shorter now. I'm fine with it, too. That means more time to eat and rest each night, and truthfully, I've been debating whether anyone could run more than sixty miles five days in a row. But I also wonder if there's a reason for the reduced race, like bloody skirmishes in the countryside or another outbreak of Ebola.

My brilliant mom came up with the original vaccine for Ebola, but since the virus continues to mutate in multiple locations, Quarrel Tayson Labs has to continually refine the vaccine to match the new strains. Still, it's completely due to my mom that these outbreaks are manageable now. Ebola used to kill thousands everywhere it erupted. These days, only a few people die.

The leopard-loin-cloth god strolls around the table,

distributing old-fashioned paper maps and handheld compasses. The other competitors stare at these items with a mix of horror and confusion. No doubt they've only used computers to plot their race courses.

"You've got to be kidding," Bash moans.

Team One, the Zimbabweans, smile smugly at each other, probably informed of this wrinkle beforehand. Those two seem like an unlikely pair of long-distance runners. The man, Rudo Lusinga, is apparently a football star, according to the accolades the announcer included when the team was introduced. The woman, Danai Mhere, is at least a runner of some sort. She was described as being on the Zimbabwean Olympic team. Coming from the same Shona tribe, they are a matched set of bookends, with close-cropped lustrous black hair, smooth dark skin, and athletic builds. They are clearly the favorites here.

Aside from the Zimbabweans, only Marco Senai shows confidence, although he double-checks the compass, holding it out on his palm to be sure it works. I do the same with mine. When our eyes meet, Marco and I nod at each other. Sometimes it pays to come from poverty and be familiar with primitive tools.

"I even looked up the declination," I murmur to Bash.

"Excellent," he says.

I wonder if he really knows what 'declination' means. As a super smart engineering student, he probably does, but then he also probably wouldn't admit it if he doesn't.

There's a bit of a lull in the presentation as the racers finger the maps and compasses and a committee of folks set up two white screens and old-fashioned projectors behind us. We have to turn in our seats to watch the side-by-side visuals as the emcee describes the race in dramatic fashion. A fat red line on a topo map leads from the start to link the three camps where we'll stay overnight, and then zigzags to the finish point at the end of the 350 kilometers. About 217 miles. So we'll run an average of more than fifty-four miles per day.

Our eyes flit from one screen to the other as images compete for attention. Pictures of rolling hills, thick forests, wide rivers, grassy plains.

"And," the emcee explains, "there is always the possibility of wild animals."

Photos of various beasts appear on the screens: lions, leopards, hippos, antelopes, elephants, crocodiles, buffaloes, baboons. As if we wouldn't have a clue what any of those looked like. But when pictures of snakes are displayed, I sit up straight and focus on each image. Slender mambas, boomslangs, cobras. Twig snakes that mimic vines and live in trees and bushes. Adders as thick as my thigh.

I swallow the anxious saliva pooling in my mouth and glance sideways at Bash. I can tell he's trying to maintain his confident expression, but his jaw is clenched.

Next come the spiders.

"Only two to watch for," the speaker explains, which sounds surprisingly reassuring after the long list of snakes. "Baboon spider and..."

Then he says something in Latin that sounds like *harper lightfoot*. Like we're going to remember that. If I see any spider, I'm going to flatten it.

He tells us both those spiders are rare.

I notice he doesn't tell us those venomous snakes are rare.

There is a recommended course to follow. The safest route, he explains. But that's not required, so of course all the competitors will do their best to find every shortcut they can to reach each checkpoint first. Often it's the ability to plot the fastest course that wins an extreme race like this.

The start times at checkpoints will be staggered according to our competitive positions, but due to the importance of arriving before dark, the winners will be determined by the sum of their times for each day.

The emcee repeats that it's *very* important to be at each checkpoint before dark. Trying to warn us about predators? Two-legged or four-legged? I'm more scared of the first kind. I understand what motivates animals. Human ambitions are often nasty surprises to me.

The slide show concludes with colorful photos of the friendly tribal villages we will encounter, and pictures of tables laden with extensive platters of food that will be served each evening.

Bash leans toward me. "I'm so glad this country is too poor for drones."

"Me, too." Each team was filmed by drones during our Verde Island race. We've both had our problems with the damn flying machines invading our privacy at home. I'd like to strip the original inventor naked and chase him around with a squadron of drones, filming him for a change, and see how he likes it.

Tomorrow, the announcer explains, is a day for adjusting

to the climate and time zone, practice runs on a nearby track, strategizing with partners, and sightseeing. In other words, we're on our own and expected to inject some tourist money into the Zimbabwean economy. He introduces a woman in a dress and high heels who can help us book tours of the area and make reservations for restaurants.

"Plans for tomorrow?" Bash asks me.

I shrug. "I don't know what I'm going to do now. Today was a total waste of time."

He lifts an eyebrow. The racer on his other side, Gretchen Vogel, leans toward Bash as she adjusts a tiny wrinkle in the tablecloth. She's listening to our conversation.

"It's complicated. I'll tell you later," I say.

The start is at seven a.m. the day after tomorrow, just a few minutes after dawn at this latitude and time of year.

As the emcee goes on and on, repeating every sentence in multiple languages, I scan the room again for white faces. There are eleven. The mystery woman from the vid is not here.

I wonder if P.A. Patterson is. Since I've never seen him, I wouldn't recognize him, unless he's sporting a neck tattoo like the ninjas who murdered my parents.

Through gaps in the crowd on the far edge of the building, I see men in military uniforms moving around. This seems ominous.

The emcee asks the crowd to part on that side of the building, and an uber-loud buzzing like a thousand enraged hornets starts up. As the people move to the sides, more than a dozen drones lift from the ground in unison, operated by the soldiers flanking them. Nearly everyone in the mess hall cheers at this display of Zimbabwean modernity. Drones will be present, the speaker tells us, to film the racers and keep us safe. The audience keeps cheering even when two of the drones collide and crash to the ground.

"I spoke too soon," Bash growls.

Where will the broadcast from those drones go? I didn't see any antennas or satellites on that old research building today. Maybe some rich people have computers or televisions, or maybe the race organizers plan to make a vid to document the race.

A huddle of men at the side of the building point at various competitors at our table and confer with a tall guy holding a clipboard. As I watch, one pot-bellied man aims an index finger directly at me and then hands Mr. Clipboard a wad of brightly colored bills.

I put my hand on Bash's wrist. "Are those guys *betting* on the race?" I tilt my head in their direction.

"W-N?" he answers. "Welcome to Africa."

When I invited X to be my partner, I didn't believe the two of us had much of a chance to win. My goal was only to get here, find that Mom Lookalike, get some answers about my family. But with Bash as my teammate, we could be winners. A spark of competitive spirit ignites in my chest. As we stand for the Zimbabwean national anthem, I wonder what the odds are against Team Eight.

Three

The sky is already changing from blue to orange in the west. As Bash and I walk to the dormitory, multicolored lights flicker on around the edges of the mess hall roof, reminding me of tacky Christmas decorations that have been left up all year long. I'm sure these lights would be described as "traditional," which seems to be an all-purpose term here to refer to everything that is from the last century. The town of Victoria Falls is called "historic," probably for the same reason.

I'm surprised when my roommate turns out to be my teammate. I'd assumed the dorms were divided by gender. But I guess it makes sense for planning purposes. Some of the other teams, like the Vogels, are husband and wife or sibling pairs. Team Eight, Dormitory Room Eight. Sebastian Callendro and Tanzania Grey.

Of course I've thought about sharing a bed with Bash. What heterosexual female wouldn't? With his lean muscular frame, dark brown hair, and those laser-green eyes he inherited from President Garrison, he's a gorgeous hunk of manhood. But I already have a hunk back home that I'm supposedly engaged to, and Emilio and I have never done the deed, so I'm definitely not starting here. And Bash has Mandy, the volunteer he worked with in New Mexico. I never met her and he doesn't talk about her, but I can tell from overhearing her chirpy voice on the phone that she's in love with my race partner.

Before we can get to sleeping or planning or anything else in this room, Bash and I need to get through tonight's dinner. The dressy dinner. I gather up my green dress and cosmetics bag and retreat to the ladies room, where I compete for mirror space with nine other women. I pull on my dress, and using a paper towel, I wipe the dust from my sandals and put them on. After twisting my hair up into a messy bun at the back of my neck, I put on my best earrings and then swipe on a little lipstick and eye shadow.

"That's as good as I'm going to get," I say to my reflection in the mirror.

The tall freckled girl looking over my shoulder wipes a finger over her lips. She's Janelle Hurst from South Africa, Team Five. That accent that sounded Australian to me is not Australian at all.

"At least you fit in," she says.

I guess she means that my skin is a shade of brown, like the other contestants, while hers is one of only three white faces. Her race partner, Andre Govender, is also from South Africa, but he's dark-skinned like the rest of us.

Did my mother feel conspicuous as a white girl growing up here? That's one of my newer vocabulary words, *conspicuous—standing out, attracting attention.* Over the last year,

Wordage has made me quite articulate.

"I don't have a tribe," I tell Janelle.

"Ah." She nods, her face solemn. "That is a pity." She leans forward to apply some mascara.

Dinner is a Zimbabwean feast, although in my opinion, it starts off a little weird, with waiters serving us tepid maize beer and dishes of tiny dried fish. The beer is *whawha*, a name that Bash and I find hilarious. The word becomes even funnier on our second glassful. The crunchy fish aren't bad if you don't look at their tiny salted heads before sticking them in your mouth. Maybe I'll convince Sabrina to serve dried sardines instead of potato chips at our next house party.

We sit behind fancy dinner plates and place cards with our names and team numbers. Photographers stroll up and down the tables, asking us to smile now and then as they flash photos. Where are all those pictures going?

We are served bowls of a delicious mushroom soup whose name I can't pronounce and tons of squash and greens and platters of crocodile tail and warthog and some thick corn mush that all the Africans dig into. I guess corn mush—they call it *sadza*—is the mashed potatoes of Africa. Personally, I think the sadza needs some salsa to add flavor. My favorite menu item is the crocodile tail, which tastes a little like lobster and feels like a nice revenge to the crocodile that tried to eat me on Verde Island. But of course, this is an African crocodile. Thinking about that, I push the meat around on my plate, arranging them so that the croc chunks form a smile beneath two eyes of sadza and a triangular nose of stewed greens.

"There could be crocodiles, Bash."

"Of course," he says. "And lions and leopards and elephants."

"I'm not worried about elephants. I understand elephants."

"Correction: You understand Bailey, Tana, not wild elephants."

I hate it when he acts older and more sophisticated like that, especially when he's right. But suddenly all I can think about is Bailey and the goats and cats and Sabrina and Aaron. I check my watch. Eight p.m. here. That means it's eleven a.m. in western Washington state, or maybe only ten. This morning. In four hours, I will be on a different calendar day than my family is. Time gets warped when you bounce from one side of the globe to the other. But I'm glad I'll have time to call when we're done eating.

"Snakes," I lob into the conversation just to provoke Bash, but all he does is nod, while my brain replays that horrific slide show. Well, that was stupid. Now I've scared myself into having nightmares tonight.

Dessert is chocolate cake, which doesn't seem especially Zimbabwean, but what do I know? Besides, I'd never pass up chocolate cake.

"You haven't seen her, have you?" Bash asks, a forkful poised beneath his mouth.

He's talking about my Mom Lookalike. "No. And the Quarrel Tayson—correction, the VF Research lab—is a slum apartment complex now."

"You already went there? Without me?"

"I didn't know you were coming, remember?"

The dark man seated on my right seems to be eavesdropping, so I bounce my eyebrows at Bash to signal him to say nothing more, and then twist in my seat to look at the fellow.

He grins at me. "I'm from the American tribe, too."

I'm astonished. He's been talking to his teammate in some other language the whole time.

"Dante Green. Las Vegas, Nevada." He holds out his hand. "Team Nine."

I shake it. "You speak...whatever that was," I say, peering around him to his teammate, who is now chatting with the man on her other side.

"My teammate is Sarah Bekele, also originally from Ethiopia. We speak Amharic," Dante informs me.

"I'm—"

"Tanzania Grey, African-American Princess of Endurance Racing," he finishes, echoing the annoying way American sports commentators usually introduce me.

And then he leans forward to study Bash. "And Golden Boy there is The President's Son, Sebastian Callendro."

It's a good reminder that I may not be as invisible here as I'd like to think.

Dante takes a bite of cake and chews as he adds, "I was adopted from Ethiopia when I was eight. Which makes me a *real* African-American."

Is he always this rude, or is he trying to psych me out? In competitions, you never know for sure. I decide to play it cool. "Good luck in the race, Dante."

"No luck needed. Team Nine is going to cream you."

Clearly this guy needs a remedial class in sportspersonship. I turn back to my cake and Bash.

The banquet doesn't end until almost midnight, so it's a darn good thing we have tomorrow off. Back in Room Eight, I'm feeling awkward even though Sebastian Callendro and I have slept in the same room together during the Verde Island race. Well, in the same tent, and then in sort of a prison cell, and in Bash's apartment, too. But my race partner shows no sign of putting the moves on me. He totally ignores me as he walks around the room, sweeping his hand along the door and window frames, checking out the light fixtures.

"What *are* you doing?" I finally ask.

"Bugs." He peers through the window blinds.

I yawn. "I saw a big cockroach in the bathroom, but the rest look pretty harmless."

"Really, Tarzan?" He shakes his head and holds out his hand to show me a little electronic gizmo. He jerks the window cord, pulling the blinds tightly shut. "All good," he concludes.

So we've slipped from equals back to worldly President's Son and impossibly naïve Tanzania Grey. I'm embarrassed that I didn't even think about electronic bugs and hidden cameras. Now I will be paranoid that things I cannot see are spying on me at all times.

"Time to plan." Bash spreads out his map on our table. "Where is Harare on this thing?"

If he doesn't remember we're in Victoria Falls, it's definitely *not* time to plan. My head is spinning from the beer, and since Bash flew in just a few hours ago, he's contending with jet lag, too. I pull the map from beneath his fingers. "Too much whawha, partner. We've still got tomorrow."

"Oh thank God." He collapses onto his bed. He hasn't even undressed, and he's snoring inside of two minutes.

I pull up the covers from each side of his bed and cocoon him. It feels good to be the competent one for a change.

My cell phone dings in my locker. I quickly retrieve it, but Bash doesn't even flinch. I'm surprised to see my caller is Kiki, the ten-year-old daughter of Marisela Santos, the woman who saved me from starving in the streets after my parents were killed.

"Hey, Lil Sis," I answer.

"Are you really in Africa?"

I laugh. "Yes. I'm in Zimbabwe."

Aaron squeezes his face in beside Kiki's. "Prove it."

That's my brother. Nothing is real for him without proof. After what he's been through, I guess I can't blame him.

"Hi, Aaron. I'm not sure I *can* prove it right now." What in this room looks African? There's really nothing special about it, it's like every dormitory room anywhere. I pace around, then peer through the closed blinds. The lights are still on inside the big tent, and servers are clearing up. That scene could be anywhere. Then a hulk lumbers across the yard between the dormitory and the mess hall, and as it rolls forward into the lights, I recognize the outline of a baboon. The huge monkey leaps onto the banquet table.

"Okay, Aaron, check this out!" I press the phone against the window pane and watch as the servers try to shoo the baboon out. It bares its teeth at them and refuses to move until one woman grabs a broom and swats the baboon on the head. Then it flees into the dark, but not before it snatches a dinner roll from the leftovers on the table.

I turn the phone back toward me. "Did that convince you?"

"Sweet!" Aaron grins. "I'll tell Bailey."

Kiki shoves him out of the frame. "This is my call, Fish Face."

"Monkey Butt!" he retorts from off-camera. My brother's going on fifteen now, but his emotional growth more or less stopped at age nine when he was kidnapped. Or maybe I just don't know a lot about fourteen-year-old boys.

"Who else is at home with you?" I ask Kiki.

The camera pans across the background of our living room, showing Marisela and Kiki's fraternal twin, Kai, watching television. Marisela blows me a kiss. Kai waves at the camera without taking his eyes off the screen. Then the face of my housemate Sabrina fills the frame. "Hi, Tana."

"Everything going okay? Bailey? Goats? Cats? Kids?" I completely trust Sabrina with our menagerie, and I'm grateful that Marisela came to stay for a few days with Kai and Kiki to help Sabrina with Aaron, but I'm pretty sure my housemate's feeling overwhelmed with three additional people in our small house. I would be, and these are my peeps, not Sabrina's.

"All okay. A little busy, but—"

Then another face crowds in beside Sabrina's. "Surprise!" blurts Emilio Santos.

Make that *four* additional people. Emilio is Marisela's nephew, an Army soldier who walks with a limp after a brutal incident in the Middle East last year. His right eye doesn't track like it should, because it's fake. I call him Shadow because he's dark and quiet and looks as if he's perpetually in need of a shave. He's also my fiancé, according to the Army. But he's never actually asked me to marry him.

Some days I can picture myself walking down the aisle with Emilio Santos. He'd be stunning in his dress uniform, and although I'm not really a dress-up kind of girl, I can picture myself in simple ivory lace or maybe a sleek satin number. I have no father to give me away, but both the Nilsen brothers could walk with me. Marisela and Kai and Kiki would be so thrilled.

My problem is that I can never envision what comes after that wedding. With my elephant and my brother, there's no way I could be a typical Army wife. The idea of trailing a soldier around the world gives me hives. But I do love Emilio and I owe him; he has protected me and comforted me all these years. And he won't be in the Army forever. When he finishes his stint and gets American citizenship, he'll want to move on to a new career. I guess we can decide on our future then.

"Hi, Shadow." I greet him with a smile. "You're on leave?"

He drapes an arm around Sabrina's shoulder. "Hanging with my fam for a few days. Aaron and I are going fishing tomorrow."

"He'll love that." I feel a tender twinge in my gut, a mix of gratitude and guilt. Gratitude for Shadow's consideration for my damaged brother, who is so hungry for adult male attention, and guilt that I never thought of taking Aaron fishing.

Shadow smiles. "*I'll* love that, too. I haven't been fishing for ages."

Then Sabrina slips away, moving out of the frame, and Shadow's lips flatten into a more serious expression. "I wanted to surprise you, Sweet Tee. Why didn't you tell me about Zimbabwe? You know that country has a really scary history, right?"

"Yeah, I know." His eyes, so dark they are almost black, are sad. That bothers me. In the past, Emilio has suffered from serious depression, and that's made him do dangerous things. But he knows me as Tanzania Grey and has no clue of my connection to Zimbabwe. I'm not going to enlighten him on a long-distance call.

So I start off with, "The government here changed recently, you know, and everyone thinks the future is bright." Then, to sprinkle a little more sunshine into the conversion, I say, "And you wouldn't believe the beautiful birds and butterflies and flowers. You don't have to worry, Shadow."

"All these dangerous races you do; I always worry about you."

Hell, *I* worry about me dying in these races, and it's nice to think that at least one other person does, too. But I have no intention of stopping.

Then he asks, "Think X is up to the challenge?"

My gut does a somersault. "Uh, about X..."

Shadow is not going to like this. But he'll find out sooner or later, so I might as well tell everyone at home now. "Xavier couldn't make it. I have a different teammate."

I turn the camera away from me and aim it at Bash's bed.

His mouth is wide open. He's snoring. He may not forgive me for sharing this view of him.

I turn the phone back around.

"Is that *Callendro*?" Shadow's eyes narrow to slits. His eyebrows dip into a scowl.

"What!?" Sabrina yelps from somewhere nearby.

"Yes," I admit. "The President's Son surprised me by showing up here today. We're Team Eight."

Shadow growls, "And you're in his room."

"It's *our* room. Teammates share a room. See?" I turn the phone away from me again and pan the room, moving slowly to show my empty bed and the running clothes I left in a jumble on it. "His bed, my bed."

"Uh-huh." Shadow slides out of the frame, and Sabrina takes the phone again.

Her gaze follows Emilio for a second, and then she turns and blinks at me, sighing.

Sorry, I mouth at her. But I say, "Tonight we had a big feast. I ate crocodile tail and chocolate cake."

"Weird."

"Yeah, it sorta was, but good, too. Tomorrow is a planning day, and then the race begins the next morning."

"Any other familiar faces there?" she asks.

I know she's asking about the Mom Lookalike, but she can't say that with everyone listening. "Only Marco Senai," I say. "I know him from the Verde Island race."

"Oh." Her gaze is wandering, distracted. I hope Shadow isn't punching holes in the walls off-screen. "Thanks for calling, Sabrina," I say aloud, then mouth *Hang in there.*

She responds, "Good luck with the race, Tana."

The rest of them join in with a shouted, "Good luck, Tana!"

"See you in a week." My heart is warm with affection as I shut down my phone. Mine may not be a typical mom-and-dad-and-siblings arrangement, but these people are still family.

I feel restless, not quite ready to join Bash in LaLa Land. After I pull my sleep shirt and shorts out of my carry-on, I leave it all on the bed and pad barefoot down the hallway. I slip out the back door of the dormitory into the dark.

It's a clear night, and the stars are bright overhead, although the security lights around our camp mess up the view of the heavens, like lights everywhere do. I'm not quite stealthy enough, and the guard standing by the back gate looks my way. He's wearing a helmet, which seems ominous. He points a finger at me, and then back toward the door.

Ignoring him, I turn my face up to the sky, hold out my arms and take a deep breath. This is my nightly ritual. No matter what the weather, I like to go out before bed and say good night to the world. It's my way of thanking the universe that I lived through another day.

Something moves in the shadows to my side. When I focus on the dark within dark, I see that I'm sharing the shadows with that thieving baboon, which is a little unnerving. I wouldn't want to be locked in the cage with the baboons at the zoo. They're strong and they're territorial, and they have long sharp canine teeth that they show off to threaten anyone who crosses them. But this one is just sitting silently, cloaked in darkness, like he doesn't want me to alert the guard that he's here. He stares up at the sky, too, and I wonder what thoughts could be passing through his monkey brain right now. After another silent moment of interspecies contemplation, I go back inside the dorm, change into my sleep clothes, and slide into my bed.

Four

Bash is still snoring when I get up at dawn, so I pull on my running gear to do a few laps around the track in the cool morning air. Marco Senai and his partner are already there when I arrive. They've set up hurdles, which they easily leap over like gazelles. Watching them, I'm pretty sure Bash and I don't stand a chance of winning, but doing hurdles is not so different than jumping over downed trees and rocks, and I've done plenty of that. Timing is everything.

In the middle of the track, two men in Zimbabwean army uniforms are fiddling with a drone and some technical-looking equipment. The drone lifts into the air, and while one man flies the machine around overhead with a handheld controller, the other watches on a tablet thingee and gives what seems like unwanted advice to the controller, based on the frown of the other man. They use their drone to follow me for a while, which is annoying. They are either inept or just plain mean, because the damn machine nearly takes off my scalp a couple of times. I decide to give up my running practice before I am beheaded.

Back at the camp, they're setting up for breakfast. Bash's bed is empty. After I shower and change, I head for the mess hall and get in line. There's a big selection of fruit and some ham and eggs, but the main offering is more corn meal mush. *Bota,* the guy beside me in line calls it this time. The Africans take big bowls of the stuff and stir in peanut butter from the smaller dishes at the side, so I do that, too, and put a dollop of some kind of purple jam on the top for good measure. Hot peanut butter and jelly mush for breakfast. It's not bad, but I add some eggs and ham to my plate.

I find Bash sitting at a table across from the South African team, so I join them and we talk about the challenges we'll face tomorrow. Janelle frets about snakes, and Andre is more worried about being ambushed by robbers.

"We won't be carrying anything worth stealing," I remind him. We'll have our packs with water and a few basic supplies. And paper maps and old-fashioned compasses.

"We will be wearing expensive shoes," Andre replies, nonchalantly licking a smear of peanut butter from his thumb. "And they will have machetes."

Bash and I exchange anxious looks.

"And Sebastian is the rich president's son," Andre adds.

I hope that Andre is trying to psych us out, but I remember the hungry looks on the faces of the kids at the slum yesterday.

"Then we'll have to outrun them," Bash says.

And I thought I needed to worry about lions.

After breakfast, we return to our room and use Bash's tablet computer and the map to scope out our route for the next four days. I have never been able to stick strictly to a plan during a race. There's always a complication that nobody predicted, like a landslide or heavy rains or a nest of killer bees. All those variables, and the fact that the competitors get to choose their routes, is what keeps these multi-day ultramarathons exciting. We always have a lot to talk about each evening, and often the racers don't know who is in the lead until we reach each checkpoint.

We determine what to take in our packs—energy gels, two-liter hydration pack, first aid basics, extra socks and an all-purpose bandanna for me. Bash hauls out the same stuff for his pack, then adds a bundle of parachute cord and a handful of lightweight carabiners. To my pile, I add my smallest Swiss army knife that has a dozen tools. You never know what might save your life or speed up your time.

Our race bibs should be pinned on the back of our running shirts, we decide, because we want our logos to show in front.

We make plans to go for a run right before dinner, when it will be cooler. Then Bash wants to know about my efforts yesterday, and I whine about the laboratory slum and not being able to find out where my mother lived.

"There are probably census or land ownership records somewhere," he speculates.

We still have the afternoon free. So, after we ask around, we end up at a crumbling stone building with a sign that grandiosely proclaims it to be the Hall of Records. My skin tingles at the anticipation of finding my grandparents and seeing where my mother grew up and maybe, just maybe, finding her there.

"Jansen?" The ebony-skinned gentleman at the desk lifts an eyebrow at my request. "In Victoria Falls?"

"Well, a little outside of it, I think, but in the area," I tell him.

"Wait here." He vanishes into a back room.

Ten minutes pass. Bash finally says, "Maybe he went out the back door to take a coffee break."

But then the clerk is back, and he holds a printout in his hands. "Yes," he says gravely, "There were several Jansens, but they are all gone now. Land redistribution, you know." His eyes meet mine when he says this, as if those words should make perfect sense to me. Then he adds, "They were white."

Since his tone manages to make that sound like a crime, I don't tell him that I am related to the Jansen family. "Is there a forwarding address for those Jansens?"

He peers at me over the top of his glasses. "Decidely not." Then he stares pointedly at Bash and states, "You are American. You cannot understand."

He manages to make that sound like a crime, too, so we peel out of there.

I want to scream in frustration. I came to Zimbabwe to find out about my mom. How could I reach a dead end so quickly? Outside the building, I take a minute to lean against the wall, my fingers in my hair, pulling on it hard. The other option is pounding my fists against the wall, but I don't want to make a spectacle out of myself.

"Where to now?" Bash asks.

"I'm out of ideas," I moan. Obviously this is yet another one of my foolish hopes that leads nowhere. "The only clues I have are photos of Mom and Dad's work parties, those chemical charts I sent you, and a couple of stupid spreadsheets."

Bash pats my arm. "Tell me what you remember. Maybe one of your memories will trigger another clue."

"Huh. Memories." I snort in disgust, releasing my hair before I tear it out. My dad was adopted and had no records about his history. I remember my mom saying she was an only child, although I also remember my dad giving her a funny look at the time, and I wondered—for ten whole seconds—what that was about.

"All I know about my mom's parents is their last name," I tell Bash. "I can't march around town and show that vid of my Mom Lookalike to random people on the street!"

He takes my hand. "That woman came to watch the previews of the race. She'll probably show up at the race, too."

That lifts my spirits a little. Maybe there's still hope.

He adds, "The good news is that now we can focus on the race. And enjoy being here, together, in Africa."

He's right, it *is* magical to be in Zimbabwe. And being with Bash makes it even more so. The thought of Shadow's jealousy flits across my brain like a bat swooping though the night, but it's quickly gone. Shadow's in the U.S. We're here.

We go sightseeing like the race organizers suggested. Bash hasn't seen Victoria Falls yet, and he insists on paying for a helicopter tour for both of us. From the air, I have to admit the view *is* magnificent. Unbelievable quantities of water fall over a cliff into a rift, like what you'd imagine the ocean would do at the edge of the world if the planet was flat like the old geezers used to think.

The local market is crowded with entertaining vendors, and after bargaining hard and trading a carabiner and a pen, I purchase a necklace made of seeds for Sabrina and an elephant-tail-hair bracelet for Aaron. Bash buys a pair of carved bookends for his mom and "real dad," as he calls him, not President Bio-Pop. Sebastian Callendro is recognized even here, though: there's a lot of murmuring and pointing and a couple of cell phones are aimed in our direction. I'm pretty sure none of those cameras are focused on me.

We go to the bridge that spans the Zambezi River, separating Zimbabwe from Zambia. We stroll from one side of the bridge to the other to step on two different African countries, and in the middle we gaze at the rapids spilling down the spectacular chasm that splits the high plateau here.

And then it's back to camp for some quick turns around the track. There are no drones this time, but Dante the Real African-American and his Ethiopian partner Sarah are doing laps. The hurdles are still set up, and when I clip one and nearly fall on my face, Dante makes a big show out of pointing and laughing.

We're supposed to attend this meal in our racing gear, so we don the clean uniforms we have saved for tomorrow, me in my Dark Horse Networks jersey and tights, and Bash with his parade of sponsor logos over his shirt and shorts. There are even more men betting in the mess hall, and when we stroll in and they see Bash's collection of sponsor logos, they line up to place more wagers, presumably on Team Eight. The poor suckers probably don't understand that most of Bash's supporters are more interested in currying favor with the ex-

President of the United States than in betting that Sebastian Callendro will get to the finish line.

On the front and back of my partner's shirt, I recognize the logos of a car manufacturer, two companies that make computer games, a soft drink company, and three sporting goods distributors. It looks like Bash has acquired several new sponsors since we ran the Verde Island Race. My eyes land on a new patch on his shoulder, a distinctive blue and silver design of an interlocked Q, T, and C.

"Wait a minute!" I point. "Isn't that Quarrel Tayson Corporation?"

He slaps my hand away, an embarrassed expression sliding onto his face. "They are funding my mining research. It could change the world."

Anyone listening might think that Bash was talking about mining for platinum or rhodium or some mineral the whole world is actively seeking. But I know he's talking about mining landfills, finding ways to recover and use all the materials buried in them.

"Change the world of garbage, you mean," I tease.

His brow furrows. "QTC recognizes that recovering the petroleum in buried plastics alone would mean a fortune."

That's no doubt true. Quarrel Tayson Corporation's tentacles extend to everything that could possibly make money. They own Quarrel Tayson Laboratories, the big pharmaceutical company Mom worked for, Quarrel Tayson Cosmetics, Quarrel Tayson Engineering, and dozens of companies that don't even bear the QT name. I can't begin to guess how many people are employed by QTC around the world, and of course everyone has Quarrel Tayson products; I use QTC face cream and sunscreen almost every day. I guess it makes sense that QTC wants to invest in landfill recovery research; we're running out of space on this planet, and mining landfills could be the next big thing. But ugh! Plowing through acres of stinking refuse...

Bash notices my disgusted expression, so he tells me, "And the recovery process could make the land usable again for farming." He probably guesses that I, the girl who used to pick crops for a living with Marisela and Emilio, would identify more with farming than with plastics recovery.

"Sorry," I say. "Just thinking about garbage."

His jaw stiffens. "I can't believe the famous Tanzania Grey is squeamish, given how she makes her living."

Touché. Bash knows that my job as a Habitat Maintenance Technician at the zoo includes hours of shoveling manure each day. And then there's Bailey, who puts out mountain ranges of poop on a regular basis. My everyday life is literally full of shit.

"Your point," I concede, using my index finger to mark a big number one on an invisible scoreboard in the air.

A small man dressed all in brown interrupts. "Sebastian Callendro!" He reaches for my partner's hand. "I am so proud to meet The President's Son."

A pained expression flits across Bash's face, but he politely shakes the man's hand.

"I am in charge of tonight's meal," the man explains. "I hope you enjoy it."

He waves us to our seats and before he leaves, acknowledges me with a slight dip of his chin. "Miss Grey."

It feels very strange to stretch a starched white linen napkin over my running uniform. Every competitor at this table must feel similarly awkward. I cast a glance at Janelle Hurst on the South African team. Her cheeks glow red as the cameras flash again and again. We are all being inspected by the other people at the sides of the room, especially the men in the betting area. We racers try to make small talk among ourselves, but I feel like a prize cow that's scheduled for auction.

A woman, dressed in what would be called a sari in India, clutches the wrist of a skinny man with a bald head. In her other hand, she clasps a toddler's fingers, and when the lump on her back moves, I realize it's another baby. As I watch, the bald man wrenches his arm away and hails the bookie. The woman turns, a disgusted look on her face, and strides out of the mess hall.

I hope these men are not stealing food from their families with these bets. If Bash and I win, will more kids go hungry or will they get new shoes? I really don't want to feel responsible for that.

Bash and I agreed earlier to take it easy on the whawha during dinner. The food is much the same as last night, with the curious addition of roast beef and Yorkshire pudding, which turns out to be a sort of bread thing, not pudding at all. I have a second helping of crocodile tail, and a huge dish of the apple cobbler they offer for desert. To my right, Dante Green the Real African-American does his best to irritate me, rehashing in great detail how I almost did a face-plant after I clipped that hurdle. What a jerk.

After dinner, my family calls me. Aaron reports that he caught two fish this morning, but he doesn't want to stab worms like that ever again. And that he's teaching Bailey to move rocks. I'm pretty sure Bailey already knows how to do that, and I'm not at all sure it's an activity to encourage, because my elephant could easily heave a stone through our living room window. But Aaron seems proud of this accomplishment and I'm not home to judge the situation, so I let it go.

Sabrina turns the phone to show me Bailey standing behind the garden fence. He's leaning into it, ripping up all the tender vines from the sweet peas I planted on the house side with his trunk and stuffing them into his mouth. But what the heck, at least he's been calm since I left, which for my elephant counts as good behavior.

As Sabrina pans the scene with her phone, I see Marisela and the twins playing a board game I don't recognize; they must have brought it with them.

"Emilio's on his way back to his job," Sabrina explains. "But he wished you good luck and said for you to remember the monarchs, whatever that means."

"I know what it means," I tell her. "Thanks."

I call Shadow's cell, but get his voicemail, and leave a message to thank him for taking Aaron fishing. I'm actually sort of relieved that I didn't have to talk to my boyfriend; sometimes it feels awkward now that we spend so many months separated from each other. Besides, my brainwaves are totally occupied thinking not only of the race tomorrow, but of the chance to see my maybe-Mom somewhere along the way.

I pull up that race promo vid on my phone and watch it again, freezing the frame each time the chestnut-haired woman looks at the camera. I know it's crazy. I saw my mother's body. I know she's dead, but I can't resist saying a silent prayer: *Please, Mom, show up.*

Sebastian sorts through his pack one last time, carefully laying out his race clothes next to mine. To me, all those corporate logos look like brands on a prize steer. My partner is owned by dozens of companies, including QTC now. My race shirt looks neglected by comparison, but at least I have only the Nilsen brothers at Dark Horse Networks to answer to. And Clark and Kent—I call them my Supermen—are friends as well as sponsors, so I want to make them proud.

"Bailey swat down any drones today?" Bash asks.

I chuckle, but I really could have done without that scary reminder that my home is often being watched.

"Is Soldier Boy still in the picture?"

I'm not sure what Bash means by that. "Emilio was visiting, but he went back to California today."

Bash inspects the inserts of his running shoes, pulling them out and then putting them back in.

"Your Bio-Pop call?" I ask. President T.L. Garrison has a habit of claiming his son whenever Sebastian might grab some media attention, and it seems like an international race would be one of those opportunities.

Bash shakes his head. "Apparently he hasn't discovered I'm here yet."

"Hence the absence of men and women in suits with receivers in their ears and weapons in holsters."

"Hence." He checks the soles of his running shoes. "Let's hope it stays that way."

"Let's." I will never forget what a pain it was to have Secret Service chasing us all over Verde Island. So far I am enjoying my relative anonymity during this competition. If The President's Son weren't my partner, I wouldn't get noticed at all.

Bash and I are in bed before ten p.m., nerves jangling in anticipation of getting up at dawn tomorrow. After I lay between the sheets twitching for an hour, I pull out my cell phone, plug in my earbuds, and watch a long video of Bailey demolishing a pile of pumpkins. I've added waltz music to the vid, and the notes pass rhythmically through my brain like ocean waves as Bailey plays, rolling the pumpkins around with his trunk. He kicks them like soccer balls and chases them as they roll away. He breaks one with his foot, and then delicately lifts each piece to his lips and gleefully chomps it with his giant molars. After Halloween, farmers give us whole truckloads of leftover pumpkins, and Bailey does this happy dance every day for a couple of months. Needless to say, autumn is Bailey's favorite time of year.

There's something mesmerizing about watching my elephant entertain himself with dozens of globular orange squashes. I finally relax enough to drift to sleep.

Five

The starter gun fires just after dawn. All ten teams are off the mark simultaneously, charging into the fierce sun rising over the scrubby plain east of Victoria Falls. Today the plan is to make approximately fifty-two miles to the first night's camp in a small village near Hwange National Park. For forty minutes, all twenty of us lope in a pack along a dirt road, surprising a couple of pickup drivers and several pedestrians trudging to market with loads of produce on their backs. The vehicles honk and plow through our midst. The people on foot step to the side of the road and stare at us, eyes wide with amazement. Exclamations follow as they see drones zooming through the sky between the racers and the vehicles behind us. A few pedestrians duck and cover their heads with their arms, which makes me wonder about their previous experiences with flying machinery.

In my other races, the organizers used professional quality drones that could fly long distances from their control stations, but the pilots of these seem to think they have to stay close by. Either the drones are only hobby quality or the pilots are inept.

It's infuriating to be pursued by a buzzing drone *and* a vehicle. I hope the landscape ahead will hold enough obstacles to keep these turkeys off our tails.

Teams begin to peel off the road, their drones and Jeeps following. Bash and I glance at each other, trying to guess when it's our turn to take our chosen route. We're used to computerized GPS wrist gizmos where you can just hold up your hand and see where you are. It's hard to read a compass and a paper topo map. It's even harder to do it when you're running. There are a billion tracks leading away from this road, wide ones made by vehicles, narrower ones made by animals or local villagers.

Finally, it's just us and four other competitors. We know the road beneath our feet leads off well to the north of where we want to end up. So Bash and I just take a guess and peel away on a trail to the right. At least away from the road there are patches of shade under scrubby trees. Those cool spots are welcome, although it's hard to see in advance what might be lurking there because the sun and shadows take turns blinding us as we dash through.

Our pesky drone follows us and the roar of the Jeep engine reverberates out of sight behind us as we trot through what looks like a farm, although not a very productive one. A tractor with two flat tires sits abandoned in a field that contains only a few scraggly stalks of corn. A half-dozen women are bent over, planting pieces of something into the dirt. Like the woman in the mess hall, some have babies sagging in long wraps tied to their backs. Kids old enough to walk are playing in the dirt beneath a big tree, and as we run past, they yell and wave. When they spot the drone above us, they shout in excitement, and the women working in the field stand up to stare, too.

Our drone buzzes above like a deviant hornet, tracking us like a hawk pursuing a mouse. Even creepier is knowing that there are human eyes somewhere peering through the drone camera from afar. Whose eyes? What are their intentions? I can't help wondering if my parents' murderers could be controlling this drone. Or P.A. Patterson. Or a terrorist tracking Bash.

Sometimes I wonder why I do these races, because these days, there are *always* drones filming the action. But I'm pretty sure that whoever killed my parents already knows all about me. Several times since I visited the Quarrel Tayson Labs in Bellingham, drones have spied on us at WildRun. I have found strange footprints and a photo from my past in the yard, and objects have gone missing from my house, which is especially frightening, a reminder that they could kill Bailey and Sabrina and Aaron and me at any time.

I've thought a lot about why they haven't. I suspect it's because they have determined that I know nothing. I can't point to any motive or to any particular person who would want to kill my parents.

Will this trip change that? P.A. Patterson may be the key to those secrets.

A thin balding man rises from behind the rusting tractor, a rifle in his hands. My brain snaps back to the present. When he swings the gun in our direction, goosebumps pop through the sweat on my neck. Are we trespassing? Have we stumbled onto some illegal operation? Were those women planting opium poppies or marijuana?

Bash and I pick up our pace, heading for the woods beyond these fields. A shot rings out. We both flinch, but then we hear a crack above our heads and a piece of metal drops from the sky. We glance over our shoulders and slow down to watch the drone wobble and sink lower behind us. Another shot, and the machine crashes to the ground, plowing into the red dirt.

The kids playing nearby shout gleefully and race toward the wreck. Bash and I keep running for the trees, but before we vanish into them, I turn and give the old rifleman a thumbs-up sign.

"What was *that* about?" I ask as we slow to a jog again. "Think they hate drones as much as we do?"

Bash shrugs and swallows some water from the tube attached to his pack strap. "Maybe The Leader used them to terrorize the population. Or maybe they've never seen one before and just shot down the strange contraption."

"I wish we could have stayed to see the pilot's reaction."

Shouts erupt behind us. Then several more gunshots ring out, interspersed by screams.

"Guess our Jeep finally arrived," Bash comments.

I try not to imagine what is taking place behind us, praying none of those bullets hit anyone. It's a reminder that we are not in a country where most obey the rule of law. Maybe shooting someone is an acceptable form of revenge here. Scary thought.

This forest is much more open than our woods in the

Pacific Northwest. Between the trees, tall mud pillars rise up like stalagmites from the ground. From nature shows on television, I know that these are termite mounds. How can anything made of wood survive in a land with so many termites that they build skyscrapers? It's mind-boggling.

Up ahead, I see the end of a black scaly tail slither into the tall grass alongside the trail. I don't want to imagine what it might be attached to, and I edge over behind Bash as we trot past the spot. We need to keep our eyes on the scenery on all sides. Anything could be out here.

As if to demonstrate this point, as we enter a small clearing, a warthog grunts to its feet and emerges from its burrow into the sunshine, waving his ugly snout from side to side to threaten us with its tusks. Bash makes a wide detour to keep the wild pig happy. I follow in his footsteps. Ahead, a handful of impala hear us coming and dart away, flashing the black M markings on their backsides. The antelopes' alarm spreads to a flock of red birds that rocket up from a stumpy tree. It's all just epic. And it's so sweet to run without the buzz of a drone overhead.

I pause to take out the map and compass, check some of the landmarks in the distance.

Bash rakes his fingers through his hair, pushing it off his sweaty brow. "We on course?"

"As near as I can tell." I check the map again, and take a sip of water from my drinking tube, then pull out my lip goop and smear some on my lips.

Bash bounces on his feet impatiently beside me. "You might not care, Tarzan, but I would like to at least place in this contest. I owe that to my sponsors."

"Thanks for the guilt trip." He's right. We both gave it our all in the Verde Island contest. I didn't plan on being a competitor here, but I know that the Nilsen brothers would certainly like me to win, or at least appear on the medal stand as one of the top three. I stash the map and compass in the pocket of my pack, take another swig of water, and then we head off again. I vow to focus and run faster, so I try to make my strides as long as possible.

After a few more miles of loping along in companionable silence, Bash says, "Ahhh." He exhales it slowly, like a happy sigh, and turns his head to toss a smile at me. "I so missed this."

I know that he means the cross-country running, but I can't resist teasing him. "Getting shot at? Or dodging warthogs and cobras?"

"Was that a cobra?"

"Could have been. I didn't want to look too close."

After several hours of surprising more antelope in the bush, we come to a river, or maybe just a big stream. Rock-strewn brown water. It's moving swiftly, but it looks no more than a foot or two deep in the middle, so we won't have to swim.

Two women are doing laundry at the edge, and several items of clothing are strewn across the bushes and rocks nearby. How they can possibly get clothes clean in such dirty water? Not far away, three young boys shout and laugh and toss rocks into the water. What is it with boys and throwing stones in water? It was one of Aaron's favorite activities when we were growing up. I could never stop thinking about all the innocent fish and tadpoles that were probably concussed by his projectiles.

"*Jambo*," I say to the women, although I suspect that may be Swahili.

Bash sticks to "Hello."

"*Mhoro*," one says.

Maybe that means hello. When I repeat it back, I earn a smile. Then another lady points to the race bib on my back.

"Eight," I say, for lack of anything more intelligent to utter.

"Aaate," she repeats, stretching out the word.

A moment of international bonding? Who knows?

We wade into the stream. The ladies gasp and chatter in their native language, and we hear the word "President" in their conversation.

Bash rolls his eyes at me. "Will I ever get my own life back?"

About halfway across, the water is up to my knees, and I'm taking care with each step to feel a safe footing between the rocks, not wanting to injure an ankle on the first day of the race. The kids are shouting louder now, so I glance their way. And then I spot what they were throwing those rocks at.

Eyes. Nostrils. A scaly tail swishes through the brown water. Sharing the river with us is ... a crocodile. It's big and it's about thirty feet away, which is a distance that a hungry croc could cross in seconds.

Six

Bash spies the monster at the same time. "Shit!"
The heck with feeling so cautiously for subsurface rocks. We race to the other bank and gallop up the slope before we stop to look back. The kids take turns shouting "Shit!" and "Eight" as they point at us, laughing. The women are doubled over, too.

"Guess *they're* used to crocodiles," Bash drawls.

I'm glad our drone was not around to film that embarrassing scene.

We stumble into a long muddy depression where dozens of orange butterflies have landed on the ground, attracted by moisture or minerals. The idea of sucking moisture seems good to me now, I have only a few mouthfuls of water left, and we still have miles to go. I squeeze some green energy gel into my mouth and use my tongue to work it over my dry teeth. As the butterflies take flight in a sunset-colored cloud around us, I can't help thinking of Emilio's parting message to me: *Remember the monarchs.*

As if he's reading my mind, my race partner comments,

"These are not monarchs."

"I know, Bash."

We run for another few minutes before he follows up with, "What's up with Soldier Boy and monarch butterflies, anyway?"

"You know how monarchs spend the winter in Mexico?"

"I've heard of that."

"It's supposed to be an incredible spectacle—thousands of monarchs, so thick around Michoacán that they break branches on trees. For years, Emilio and I have promised each other that we will go together to see that."

"Ah." He and I jog for another few seconds, and then Bash comments, "That's a sweet dream."

"Yes, it is." I like to think it's more than a dream. Our plan to go to Mexico together gave us hope in hard times, and I still want to believe Shadow and I will do it. But since I've befriended Sebastian Callendro, *remember the monarchs* sometimes sounds like a warning when Shadow says it.

I know that Marisela and the twins expect me to marry Emilio, but I don't like anyone trying to constrict my future. I'm plenty good at limiting my options all by myself. But I do care for that boy-man-soldier, and now he's lost an eye and has terrifying nightmares. Emilio needs all the love he can get to face his own future. And what would Marisela think if I broke things off with her nephew? Would I lose my foster mother, and my adopted siblings Kai and Kiki, too? I couldn't bear that.

I'm pretty sure that last year my housemate Sabrina was developing feelings for Emilio, but now she seems a little scared of him after being the target of one of his PTSD attacks last year. I don't blame her. Spending time with Emilio these days is like knowing you're storing unstable explosives in your attic; a blast could rip your world apart at any time.

That's what it's like to live with my brother every day, too. Each morning I have to look deep into Aaron's eyes to make sure that my little brother is looking back, and not Jaime Ramirez, the psychotic junior criminal Aaron was for four years.

I'm so busy thinking about my screwed-up family life that I would have missed the giraffes if Bash hadn't pointed them out. How can giraffes be nearly invisible like that in the forest? They blink their long lashes at us as we run past, and I feel guilty that I have let my mind wander when I should be appreciating each step in this incredible landscape. A little further on, we surprise a group of Guinea fowl. Back home, these are tame chickens, but here they are wild birds, kind of like our ptarmigan or quail.

I am parched. I swallow the last ounce of water in the pack on my back and try to hold it in my mouth as long as I can before swallowing it. Bash has to be in the same predicament; I haven't seen him use his drinking tube for miles now, and his lips look so dry they're about to crack.

When we cross a two-wheel track that's heading in the right direction, we decide to follow that, and as we pass a sign to Hwange National Park, we see two runners about to converge with our course. It's Team Nine, Dante and Sarah, the Ethiopian-Americans. A drone catches up with us. Bash and I pour on the speed for the last three miles, leapfrogging Team Nine twice and dashing into camp only a second ahead of them.

Unlike other international competitions, this primitive race has no drug tests or medical exams at the end of the day. I guess any team here could be using an illegal performance enhancement drug if they knew where to get it. Which makes me suspicious of the Zimbabwean pair, who were lounging and sipping cold glasses of a red drink as we staggered and collapsed after passing the official checkpoint. They didn't even look as though they'd run a mile, let alone more than fifty. I can't wait to see their drone footage.

I'm thinking about all this as I shower in rustic conditions, standing on a raised mat with a bucket of tepid water pouring onto my head, surrounded by walls of thin sticks that come up only to my shoulders. My leg muscles are twitching. My feet ache. All I can think of is dinner and sleep.

Then a woman walks past.

A woman with chestnut-colored hair.

Seven

By the time I towel off and shimmy into my clean shirt and shorts, the woman has vanished. The village is small, consisting of round stick huts with thatched roofs arranged in a pattern that radiates out from one rectangular cement-block structure. The whole place is surrounded by a high fence made of interwoven thorny branches. Judging by the amount of cow dung ground into the soil I'm walking on, I'd guess the villagers typically keep their cattle inside the fence at night. Now there's not a cow in sight. Instead, there are trucks with water tanks or heavy generators on their beds, tethered to the rectangular building by hoses and electrical cables that snake across the ground. There's also a van with a huge satellite dish on the top and the letters Z-TV painted on its sides. We are all locked inside the fence, which makes me feel like a captive cow. Or maybe an orphan calf, searching for her mother.

Bash and I have been assigned to a small hut with two hammocks and a lantern that hangs from the ceiling between them. I don't return there, but instead stride quickly around the whole area, peeking into buildings. A feast is being laid out in the rectangular building. I see a long table covered in cloth in the colors of Zimbabwe A young woman is setting out plates on it, and another table already holds a bounty of covered dishes. My mouth fills with saliva and my stomach growls.

I pass several more huts, observe more of my fellow competitors through the open windows and doors than I really want to—a pair of naked butt cheeks and a flash of breasts as the South Africans change clothes. A startled glance from the half-dressed Germans when they see me gazing into their space.

That chestnut-haired woman. She can't have simply disappeared! I pass out of the competitor zone and into the area of the villagers' huts, walking quickly, peering through doorways. The interiors of these huts could not be more primitive, with fire pits on the floors, a few bowls on shelves and clothes dangling from hooks. Woven sleeping mats instead of hammocks. These people have nothing.

Most huts are empty, but in one that is more oval than round, I see at least twenty people crowded around a cooking fire. They look up from the pot on the fire and stare at me through the smoke. The smallest kids are nearly naked and have their fingers in their mouths. Their vacant expressions make me wonder if these villagers are hosting the racers by choice. And where are their cattle? I hope they're safely penned up somewhere nearby.

Their gaze abruptly darts away from mine, back to their cook pot. Then a hand clamps onto my forearm, startling me.

"Miss," growls the scrawny brown man attached to the hand. I have to hunch over a bit to see his eyes, because he's shorter than I am and he's wearing a helmet.

"You are lost," he states. "I will take you to your hut."

A red armband proclaims him to be STAFF. But what's with the helmet? He has a machete shoved through a loop on his belt, too. So I guess he's some sort of guard. The strength with which he tugs on my arm leaves me little choice but to follow him back to the competitors' area.

"I thought I saw a woman with reddish brown hair," I explain. "She looked like someone I know."

"Perhaps you mean her." He points to the Z-TV van, where the chestnut-haired woman is standing, talking to a dark-skinned cameraman.

Damn. I was too focused on the hair. She's shorter and younger than Mom, and her skin is as brown as mine. Not Mom. Not even close.

"Here we are." His hand finally leaves my arm as we stop in front of a hut with a large number eight on a cardboard sign above the door.

"Thank you," I tell my guide or warden or whatever he is.

"Dinner in twenty minutes." He flashes his teeth in what is probably supposed to be a smile.

Inside the hut, I find Bash lounging in his hammock, his hair still wet and slicked back from his shower. He raises an eyebrow. "In trouble already?"

"I thought I saw her," I explain, then shake my head. "Same hair, but not her."

"Could this one be the woman in the vid?"

"Negative. The one here is African." Wait, my Mom was African and she's white. "I mean, this woman has dark skin, so

I assume she's local." Which also might be a big assumption. Heck, that woman could be American, or British, or...

"There's still time." Fortunately, Bash is not paying attention to my mental meanderings.

I shrug, try to sit down in my hammock, and nearly fall out the other side. Bash is still teaching me a proper hammock-entering technique when the dinner bell rings. My thigh muscles are screaming when I roll out of my string bed, and Bash is walking like he's made out of badly matched spare parts, too. We both get excited when we see big pitchers of whawha on the tables.

After a long series of fits and starts, the staff gets enough of its act together to show some of the drone video from today. Most of the footage features the Zimbabwean team, who trot easily along a dirt road, not even breaking a sweat. They are in first place right now. Clearly, they have inside knowledge of the terrain. The staff makes a big show of bringing them a second pitcher of whawha and a gigantic helping of pineapple cake, and the chestnut-haired television reporter interviews them at the table.

In second place is Team Three, Marco Senai and Hasina Okeke from Kenya. I'm not surprised. Marco is a racing machine. If everyone has an equal chance, I bet Team Three will win the Extreme Africa Endurance Challenge.

The Germans are in third place and seem very smug about it.

Surprisingly, Bash and I are in fourth place, and when they show the clip of Team Eight beating Team Nine by mere seconds, Dante Green the Real African-American aims his half-filled glass of whawha in my direction and tells the whole table that was a total fluke and will never happen again.

All teams are in camp tonight, but a runner from each of three teams is limping badly, so we'll see who sets off tomorrow. We probably won't know how many are still competing until we reach camp tomorrow night.

I keep my cloth napkin in my lap throughout dinner, and I tuck rolls and fruit and little hard cheeses into it. I think about adding some of the buffalo meat we receive, but it's too drippy. At the end of the meal I have nowhere to hide my bundle, so I just hold it down by my side and hope it's not too visible as all the racers exit together. Bash, however, notices and gives me a lifted eyebrow, and the guards watch as we stroll back to our hut, shaking their heads. I hear the word *baboon* in their conversation. Either they are calling me by that name because I'm stealing food to eat later, or they believe my stash of goodies will attract one of the thieving apes to our hut.

I wait until the guards turn away and then I slip out and walk back to that oval hut I studied earlier. Only two people are inside now. A tired-looking middle-aged man with a jagged scar parting the close-cropped hair on his scalp sits on a stool as a bent white-haired woman sweeps the dirt floor around the dying fire.

"*Jambo*," I say to both of them, giving each a little bow. "*Jambo*."

I really need to learn the right word for hello in Shona, which is the most common native language here. When I hand my bundle to the old woman, she inspects it, then regards me solemnly with reddened eyes. I can't tell if she's grateful, or insulted, or angry, but she dips her head in acknowledgment. The man extends an index finger and points to the doorway. As I exit, I hear the old woman calling to someone. Her tone sounds cheerful.

A guard catches up with me a few huts down, chattering like an angry jay. I can't understand a word he's saying. He follows me back to our hut.

Bash is tucked into his hammock, studying our map in the glow of his headlamp. "Welcome back, Robin Hood," he says without looking up.

"Good evening to you, Maid Marian."

He raises his eyes, purses his lips, and pats the hair around his right ear in a gesture reminiscent of old Marilyn Monroe films. "I've been waiting for you, darling."

This is what I love about Bash. He's so easy to be with. Emilio—Shadow—is definitely not easy. But is that because I've told Bash my whole history, while Shadow knows me only as secretive Tanzania Grey? Is it fair to compare the two of them when only one knows the real me?

There's no way to sort that all out tonight; I feel like I sprained my brain just pondering it for a minute. Grabbing my own headlamp, I position myself at his side. "Have you planned our route for tomorrow?"

We spend a half hour doing just that, but sleep is fast overcoming both of us. Soon we're yawning more than focusing, and when I point out a landmark to Bash, I get a strangled snort in response. My partner's eyes are closed. I switch off his headlamp and pull the map from his hands.

When I go out to say goodnight to the world, the helmeted

guard guy follows me. He tries to stick to the shadows, like that would render him invisible. It's creepy, so I don't walk far away from our hut. Stars twinkle overhead, but dark clouds are stacking up in the east.

"Are storms coming?" I ask my human shadow.

He doesn't respond. Still pretending to be invisible.

Night sounds rise in the darkness outside the fence, noises I can identify only because I've worked in the zoo after dark. Some sort of big antelope or buffalo is huffing, and then I hear the quick rising whick-whick-whick that I used to think came from a hyena, until I actually witnessed a zebra make that sound. A big cat roars in the north, and then one answers from the south.

"Stereo lions?" I murmur.

The guard still doesn't answer, but I hear the rustle of clothing as he shifts position.

Bash is snoring in his hammock when I go back. Our duffel bags have been stashed in the hut with us, so I check my cell phone and I'm amazed to find that there is service here, probably due to the satellite dish on the TV news van. Sure enough, according to the weather site, there's a possibility of thunderstorms tomorrow. Lovely. In my email, there's an encouraging message from Shadow: *Run, Tana, run!* Maybe he's over his snit about me partnering with The President's Son.

Then a chime announces another message, forwarded from Dark Horse Networks.

See you soon.

- P.A. Patterson.

Eight

Patterson's name raises the hair on the back of my neck every time I see it. I remind myself that the invitation to this race came from Patterson, so I should not be surprised that he knows I'm here. But the message is disturbing: *See you soon.*

Cyberstalkers rarely show in person, I've been told. I try to take comfort in that and move on, but a niggling voice in the back of my mind asks how I would know this P.A. Patterson if he were standing right in front of me.

I can't get the image of Phineas Pederson, the intimidating chief of security at Quarrel Tayson Labs, out of my head. He's uber creepy. He snapped a photo of me when I was sleuthing around in Bellingham, and I swear he plotted to whack me with a canoe paddle during the Ski to Sea Race, too. After Bash discovered Pederson was formerly a partner at Tyrol Operations, a mercenary organization that has been accused of war crimes, I've always wondered: Is Phineas Pederson pretending to be P.A. Patterson? Is he one of the two ninjas I saw standing over my parents' bodies?

I study the entryway of our hut, which has no door. The windows have no glass. Anyone or anything could just slip or slither in. Indeed, something is moving right now along the windowsill closest to my hammock. I flip my headlamp in that direction and highlight a small lizard. The creature—I think it's a gecko—is quite pretty, with a green head and a rainbow-colored body. Alarmed by the light, the reptile quickly vanishes, slipping outside again.

Who or what else might creep in while we are sleeping?

There are guards, I remind myself.

But would they suspect P.A. Patterson was a threat? Might they be in league with him?

Stop it, stop it, stop it, Tana! I will never get to sleep if I keep this freight train of anxious thoughts rumbling along.

I try to switch my brain onto a more logical track: Phineas Pederson may seem threatening, but you don't know for sure that he wants to hurt you. You have no proof that Pederson is Patterson. And you have zero evidence that P.A. Patterson wants to harm you. You've received only gifts and encouraging notes from him.

If only I could find that woman from the promo vid. That's why I came to Africa. I take a deep breath. Africa. An enchanting place. *Yes, celebrate that.* I take ten deep slow breaths as I review the wonderful things we saw today. Giraffes. A warthog. Impala. Butterflies. Orange wings opening and closing. Emilio. Monarchs. Something to look forward to, seeing the monarchs in Mexico.

Geographastic tells me that the Kalahari Desert stretches across Botswana, Namibia, and parts of South Africa. I resolve to look for it when we fly back across the continent. Wordage teaches me *epochal—extremely important, especially significant, without equal.*

I'm starting to feel drowsy. I return to my email messages.

Bailey misses you is the word from Aaron, and Sabrina reports that everything is okay back home. This should make me feel relieved, but for some reason it makes me feel like nobody needs me there. I decide to chalk up that depressing emotion to exhaustion. I can no longer keep my eyes open. I crawl carefully into my hammock, rolling myself in my blanket like a burrito, wondering about the odds of rolling over and falling out during the night.

Nine

The wind is blowing when we get up on Day 2 of the race. Bash and I quickly dress and gear up, check our route, and head for the mess hall to await our start time. The Zimbabweans on Team One are already gone, and the media van is gone, too, which may or may not be coincidental. My muscles are stiff, but I know that will pass once we begin to run. We are stuffing our faces with banana pancakes and sausages and fruit when in stroll two men who are obviously and embarrassingly American. They're dressed in pale blue guayabera shirts over khaki pants, but their postures are so stiff they might as well be wearing suits and ties.

With his fork halfway to his mouth, my partner takes one glance at them and says, "Crap."

"Good morning, sir," the tallest one says.

"There's no need for you to be here," Bash growls. He's managed to evade them for nearly a year by hiding under an assumed name in rural New Mexico, but obviously he hasn't totally escaped Secret Service surveillance.

"We were requested by your father," the shorter bearded

one responds, then murmurs quietly, "It's a dangerous country. I'm Lyman, sir."

"Pratt," says the other.

Both Lyman and Pratt have black skin, which makes me wonder what percentage of the U.S. Secret Service is African-American. These two were no doubt picked so that they'd be unobtrusive, but those shirts are not typical African wear. The bulges of the holsters under them aren't, either.

Other competitors are in here eating. Every eye in the room is staring at these guys. The secret stiffs arrange themselves behind Bash, who rolls his eyes and mouths *Sorry* at me.

While it's a pain to be followed everywhere, after P.A. Patterson's message last night, I don't regret these two being here. Their mission is to protect The President's Son, but as his race partner, that radius of protection will include me as long as I stick close.

When Bash and I walk outside to stretch and warm up, the stiffs follow us. At the corner of the building, two men in Zimbabwean army uniforms are tinkering with a drone on a table and bickering with each other.

A scent of smoke hangs in the air. "Is the smoke from campfires?" I ask.

The soldiers frown at me, annoyed by the interruption.

"Farmers clear their fields before the dry season," one finally responds.

It already seems pretty darn dry here to me, but I've been told it's actually an in-between month with a chance of rain nearly every day. The air feels humid even while the landscape is growing parched.

The soldier turns back to the drone. He motions the other soldier to stand back, and taps something on the tablet he holds. The drone buzzes and dances across the table. The other guy manages to grab it an instant before it falls to the ground. Then they begin to argue again.

"Five minutes," one of the race organizers says to Bash.

The soldiers overhear and start yelling at each other, gesturing to the drone and to Bash and me. I deduce that the nonworking machine is meant to be our mechanical guardian today, and Bash and I share a smile.

We do a few quick stretches and strap on our packs. A whirring whine accompanies the sleek silver drone that lifts into the air and quickly disappears into the sunrise above. It's obviously a superior stealth machine, able to fly higher and quieter than the drones used by the Zimbabweans. Our non-bearded secret squirrel, Pratt, smirks at us as he moves his fingertip across the tablet he holds.

Then he gazes meaningfully in the direction of the African soldiers. "The U.S. will provide drone protection for Team Eight," he announces.

Lyman folds his arms, a smug expression on his face.

The Zimbabweans glare back.

"Video?" One snaps off the word, his jaw locked.

"We'll see," Lyman responds, his gaze steely.

Yeesh. International weenie wagging. I guess Team Eight doesn't get to vote. Bash rolls his eyes again, leans my way, and says in a stage whisper, "Maybe this drone will get shot down, too."

Lyman and Pratt's haughty expressions shift toward annoyed.

"Team Eight, time to run," says the race organizer, waving the tiny Zimbabwean flag she holds in her hand.

So we do.

At least we don't have a Jeep roaring on our heels again as we lope down the dirt road leading out of the camp. We follow that easy track for about ten kilometers, then turn off to take a shortcut through the bush to the north and our next checkpoint. Although our drone is sufficiently sophisticated to fly high enough above us that we can't hear it, we occasionally catch a glimpse of sunlight glancing off something in the sky. Bash keeps apologizing.

"Forget about it," I tell him after the fifth 'I'm sorry.' "I know it's not your choice." Personally, after that *See you soon* message last night, I'm glad we have an electronic observer.

For the first two hours, we jog down dirt roads through farms that have seen better days. Although I see a few rows of squashes and corn and some trees with tiny green fruits, many fields have been abandoned to weeds that even the skinny cows and goats don't seem interested in eating. Shacks made of scrap wood and metal dot the landscape, most with ragged clothes dangling from clotheslines. One clothesline close to the road has a dozen long strips waving in the wind, and when we get closer, I see those are snake skins. Most are slender and black or brown, but one is gigantic, with a beautiful pattern that matches Moses, a massive African rock python at the zoo where I work. I can't say that I'm a fan of serpents, but they can't help being snakes, and they deserve to live like everything else. When a man stacking wood nearby notices us looking at the skins, he shakes his fist at us.

Many of the shacks have at least one human sitting outside, and most of these people seem to be completely idle. Skinny farm dogs dart out to the road to threaten us, baring their teeth and growling, but it's easy to tell their hearts are not really into confrontation. If we had time, I'd stop and befriend the black one that looks like my old dog, Joker.

Now and then, kids race out to the road and run alongside us for a few hundred yards, laughing and chattering in a native language. They look ragged and thin, but they seem reasonably happy.

Clearly, this is no longer the heavenly homeland that my mother raved about, a paradise to grow up in. Besides the dogs, the only non-livestock animals we see in the morning are birds—a few Guinea hens along the road, and several flocks of brightly colored fliers—maybe bee-eaters?—winging overhead. It seems wrong to be running through an African country and not see wild animals. This area is hot, dusty, and filled with way too many humans.

So when we finally enter a forest, I feel relieved. The trees are not particularly tall, but the canopy is thick enough that our drone will have problems spying on us beneath. The shade is welcome, but it takes a while for our eyes to adjust, and now, instead of worrying about what happened to all the wild animals, I worry that predators could be lurking here in the shadows. And frankly, I don't want to see a giant python outside of a cage.

Bash and I are running on a narrow trail that leads more

or less in the direction we want to go. It might be more precise to take a shortcut, but the surrounding brush looks like slow going, with a lot of thorny bushes, so I hope to make good time along this path and then zag back to the precise compass heading we need when the shrubbery decreases.

The drone whines overhead. It's probably flying low now, searching for us. We can't see it, and the noise soon fades away.

I want this to be a manmade trail, not a game trail, so when I see a small group of people ahead, I feel vindicated by my choice. I count six men, loitering by the sides of the trail, eating lunch. Workers? We are in their midst before I have chance to think too much about where they might have come from. They put down their food and rise to their feet. Two men step into the path ahead of us, blocking the trail, and only then do I notice that they hold machetes in their hands.

Ten

Bash and I turn to retreat, only to encounter another man behind us, aiming a rifle at Bash's chest. He says something unintelligible, then holds out his hand and waggles his fingers. His tone is threatening.

My sweaty skin turns cold and prickly. Bash tries to put on a brave face, but the stiffness of his jaw tells me he is terrified, too.

Is this what P.A. Patterson meant by that *See you soon* threat? Will we be beheaded right here? I scan the necks of these guys, looking for flying birds or waves, those V-shaped tattoos that I saw on the neck of one of my parent's killers.

No tattoos. And these guys are all dark-skinned, whereas my parents' tattooed murderer was white.

The thugs speak in a native language, and they clearly all know each other. Their weapons are not sophisticated. These are most likely the thieves that South African racer Andre predicted. What do they think we could be carrying in the midst of a race? We hold out our hands, showing that we have nothing. I pray they don't recognize Sebastian. It can't occur to them how valuable The President's Son might be.

The whine sounds again overhead, and everyone glances up at the thick branches ahead. Then the sound fades as the drone moves away, and our attackers focus all their attention on us again.

"Pull out your pockets," Bash suggests, pulling the pockets of his shorts inside out.

"I have no pockets." I pat my hips and shirt to show that.

The men's faces show disgust at our display, and my fear intensifies. Life is cheap in Africa. Women are raped. Unexplained bodies turn up in too many places.

The gun wielder growls and gestures to our packs, then our shoes. Andre was right; they'd even steal shoes. Now I fervently wish our drone could see through the branches overhead.

I decide to pretend that I have no clue what's going on. When confronted by treacherous men, I've found the ditsy woman routine sometimes works.

"*Jambo*," I say, turning to smile at each man in turn. There are three flanking us, plus one behind and two ahead. Only one has a firearm, but the other five have machetes, which I know can be every bit as lethal. "*Jambo*, friends! We are Team Eight, in the Extreme Africa Endurance Challenge."

Bash darts a sideways glance at me that suggests I've lost my mind.

I feel a hand crawl onto my shoulder from behind and I cringe away, but then the man grabbing me flicks off my baseball cap with an upward slap of his hand. I swivel to focus on his face, and we stare at each other for a long second. A jagged scar zigzags through the close-cropped hair on his scalp. This is the same man I saw at the camp last night, in the hut when I gave the old woman the food. His eyes widen. He remembers me, too.

"*Mira!*" he growls, signaling to the rifleman with a sharp wave of his hand.

It sounds like a command, but the other guy only frowns at him.

"*Mira!*" he says again, turning to glare at the other men.

In Spanish, that word would mean "Hey!" or "Look!", but it obviously means something else here. An angry argument erupts around us, and some of the men wave their machetes as they gesture. I can't understand a single word, but Scarhead is obviously trying to convince the others. I'm worried about what he's going to persuade them to do. Does he know who Bash is? Is he telling them to drag me off into the bushes and take turns? It's terrifying to have knives and a gun pointed at you. It's even more horrific when you can't understand the intentions of your attackers.

I try to keep my expression innocent, but I'm pretty sure I look scared stiff. Bash's expression wavers between frightened and angry, and I worry that he's about to make some heroic gesture that will get us both killed.

Then the argument abruptly stops, and the circle of thieves simply backs away from the trail. Scarhead gestures with his machete, indicating we can continue.

It seems too good to be true, and as I quickly snatch my cap from the ground, I expect to feel a blow. As soon as I have my cap in hand, I run. Bash is right behind me. Fearing another ambush ahead, we don't talk, but only sprint as fast as we can, trying not to trip when we glance back over our shoulders. After we've put at least a mile between ourselves and the goons, we stop to wet our dry throats and gulp down some energy gel.

"What just happened?" Bash asks after he catches his breath. "At first I thought it was a robbery, then I thought for sure it was going to turn into another kidnapping."

He's referring to an incident during the Verde Island race in which he was the target. We were both lucky to get out of that predicament alive.

"No," I tell him. "For once it wasn't about you, Sebastian." I tell him about Scarhead and the food I gave the old woman the night before.

"Well, bless your little soft heart." He leans over and gives me a surprise kiss. "You saved us."

"They're just going to lie in wait for the next people to walk through," I point out.

"Nothing we can do about that. Let's hope nobody else comes this way today."

We debate for a minute about whether to continue along our path or attempt to cut through the thick brush on a more direct compass heading. We're both anxious about meeting more robbers on this trail, but even more worried about being killed by thugs with guns if they think we're some sort of animal crashing through the woods. They seem like types who would shoot first and bury their mistakes later.

After a few more miles, we see an opening ahead. Just before we get there, a warthog steps into the trail. It stares at us for a long minute, as if it can't believe its little piggy eyes. With protrusions and sharply curved tusks and wayward tufts of hair, this is a face only a mama warthog could love; farm hogs are handsome by comparison. It tosses its head once, snorting, and then trots off into the trees on the other side. Then I realize this *is* a mama warthog, because Bash and I have taken only a couple more steps when five fuzzy little piglets dash across the path, following the big one, their tails held high in the air.

"Adorable," Bash says, his tone implying the opposite.

That's pretty much the sum total of the wildlife for the day. When the Zambian team limps into camp at sunset sans packs and shoes, we realize the robbers were the most dangerous creatures along the route today. Bash and I are still in fourth position, and I regret that there wasn't some way to warn all the teams behind us.

Our drone located us again shortly after we exited the forest, but of course Pratt and Lyman had no clue what had transpired while we were out of sight.

Tonight the camp is an actual game lodge, albeit a fairly rustic one. Each team is assigned to a tent on a wooden platform. Our Secret Squirrels have already arrived. They commandeered the tent next to ours, which gets the teams all out of sequence, but agents Lyman and Pratt don't seem to care. Inside our tent, I'm relieved to see cots instead of hammocks. There are separate toilets and solar-heated showers, a central mess tent with solar-powered lights, and internet service. I send a quick message to Sabrina, Aaron, Marisela, and Emilio to report that we've survived another day.

Wordage gives me *acquit*, which at first I think is a waste because everyone knows it means *to get a verdict of not guilty in court.* But then I discover the word can also mean *to perform or behave in a specified way.* Hmm.

Geographastic tells me that Timbuktu is a World Heritage Site in Mali, which is news to me. I thought that place name came from a novel.

This camp is run by a South African tour company. There's no *whawha*, but there is cold canned beer, and my aching body feels better after having two of those, not to mention wolfing down a huge plate of food and a massive amount of mango pudding. As we're leaving the mess tent after the usual banquet, the manager, a Boer type with blond hair and a deep tan, stands beside the door, wishing us all a good evening. As I pass, I notice the nametag on his uniform shirt says *Rob Jansen.*

Eleven

I point at the manager's nametag. "Jansen! We may be related."

"Really?" He eyes me: black hair, café au lait skin, as compared to his deep tan and sun-bleached blond coiffure. "How so?"

I can't talk about my relatives in front of the other competitors because the story I tell the public is that my dad is from Tanzania, and that's where I got my name. I tell Bash I'll catch up with him in our tent. The not-so-Secret Squirrels follow him down the walkway. I wait until the other racers all pass out of the mess hall before I tell Rob Jansen that some of my mother's side of the family were Jansens from Zimbabwe, adding. "I think I may still have cousins here somewhere."

He smiles. "The Jansens are a prolific bunch. Over the years we spread out over the globe."

Finally, I feel a spark of hope. Maybe Rob and I are third cousins or something. Maybe he's heard of Mom.

He suggests I come to his tent and he'll use his cell phone to look up his family tree, get the names of the Jansens who live in Zimbabwe. He compliments me on being fourth in the race, and he says he likes my dress.

Tonight I put on that slinky green thing again. Our footsteps echo hollowly as we walk along the raised wooden walkway. The boards are not precisely level, and when I catch the toe of my sandal on one, he puts a guiding hand on my back over the spot where my dress straps crisscross. His fingers are warm on my bare skin in the cool evening air, and I know that the tingling sensation they raise are causing two of the firefly tattoos across my shoulder blades to light up.

"Sorry about the robbers you encountered on the trail," he commiserates. "Not a proper intro to Zimbabwe." He pauses briefly, then adds, "But unfortunately, a common event here."

When we reach one of the outermost tents, Rob pulls aside the flap and gestures for me to precede him.

Inside the tent, there's a cot and a small desk with a lockbox bolted to it. Rob points to the cot. "Have a seat. Keef tats, by the way."

"Keef?" At least I think that's what he said. I sit on the edge of the cot.

"Nice," he translates for me as he lets the tent flap fall shut. He presses some buttons on the lockbox, opens it to extract a cell phone.

"Thanks. They represent my family." Three small fireflies are tattooed across my upper back. Two of them light up with special fluorescent ink when I get especially hot or when I'm angry or scared. Those two represent the glowing spirits of my parents, and the third non-fluorescent firefly was for my brother, because when I got the ink, I didn't know if Aaron was alive or dead.

After turning on the phone, Rob raises his face to meet my gaze. "Which Jansen did you say you're looking for?"

Good question. I decide to give him Mom's maiden name. "I have one cousin named Amy Jansen. But she's in the States now. So I'm looking for any Jansens who are still here. White Jansens."

"Right." He nods and swipes around on his phone for a bit. Then he comes over to the cot and sits down beside me, his thigh touching mine as he leans close to show me the phone screen.

The text is too tiny to read. I take it from him and use my thumb and forefinger to enlarge the display. It's just a list of links, and most have nothing to do with Jansens. As I'm perusing them, Rob clamps an arm around my shoulders, then bends his head and nuzzles my neck.

"Uh." I use my shoulder and elbow to try to shift him away. "Thanks, but no thanks, Rob. I'm not interested."

He hooks a finger under my dress strap and slides it down over my shoulder.

"No, really." I slide the strap back up and try to focus on the screen again. "We might be cousins. And I have a boyfriend."

"He's not here, is he?" He pulls down the strap again, this time revealing most of my left breast, and then he shoves me backwards on the cot, one hand on my shoulder. His other hand creeps up my thigh between my legs. "You know you want it."

His eyes are half closed as he plants his mouth on my lips, grinding his face into mine.

I still have his cell phone in my right hand, so I try to push him away with my left. The hand between my legs moves higher.

The time for polite refusals is past. I snake my left arm between his neck and mine and abruptly jam my forearm against his throat. When he breaks his lip-lock on me, I raise my head and throw his cell phone as hard as I can toward the desk. I am gratified to see it crack hard against the corner of the metal safe and then bounce onto the floor.

"You little bitch!" He shoves me down again and throws a leg over mine, climbing on top of me.

This guy clearly does not know who he's tangling with. I fist my right hand and punch him as hard as I can at the edge of his left eye, and then, when he rears back howling, I follow that with a quick left to the jaw and then I raise my leg and roll, bucking him off onto the floor.

Before he can get up again, I'm off the cot. He grabs my left ankle, but I kick him hard in the ribs with my right foot. His fingers drop away, and I push out of the tent.

My dress strap is torn from the bodice, my face is flaming, and I'm outraged as I stride to the tent Team Eight has been assigned. I'm furious with Rob Jansen, but I'm also livid with myself for falling into the oldest trap in the world. That was an act of epochal stupidity. And I still have to spend the night here in the same camp with that lech. I'm glad I'm sharing sleeping quarters with Bash.

The flap on our tent is closed, but the canvas is lit up from within. I pause for a few minutes outside, taking deep breaths, staring upward at the skies as I try to cool off. I'm grateful to be alive, I'm grateful to have escaped from Rob Jansen, but this has not been a day that I'm especially thankful for.

I am such a fool. This was—is—such a stupid wild goose chase. And if Rob Jansen truly is a cousin of some sort, maybe I don't want to meet the rest of the Jansens. One of the Secret Squirrels comes to the doorway of the next tent. Lyman is dressed in the same clothes I saw him in earlier, and he scrutinizes me for a long moment. Then he glances quickly in the direction of Rob Jansen's tent, and I realize he probably watched me walk down there.

I give Lyman an OK sign with my index finger and thumb, while realizing that this common American sign means "asshole" in many parts of the world, maybe even here in Africa.

Why are so many men scumbags?

Lyman nods and goes back into his tent, letting the flap close behind him.

The camp is quiet now, with the competitors and most staff settled down for the night. A few guards stroll around the perimeter, shadows in the night. Most tents along the walkway are already dark, and now that the blood has stopped pulsing through my skull, I hear lions roaring back and forth to each other, audibly marking their territories. And then a hyena's cackling call. Some of the magic of Africa seeps through my fog of anger, and after admiring the unfamiliar stars here for a few moments longer, I slip into our tent.

Bash is reading. He holds an actual printed book in his hand. My torn strap falls over my shoulder, dangling down the front of my sundress as I rummage through my duffel for my sleepwear.

He politely turns away as I begin to unzip, but over his shoulder, he quietly says, "Do I need to hit someone?"

I smile to myself. "Thanks. I already took care of that."

As I slip into bed, he rolls onto his back again and sets his book on the table by his bed. "Seven hours to wakeup call," he informs me. "We could still win, Tana."

"Sadly, you have an idiot for a partner."

Sebastian Callendro doesn't deserve my lack of focus. Neither do the guys at Dark Horse Networks. I am supposed to be a professional. No more Jansen hunting. Only racing from now on. Before Bash can respond, I add, "But from now on, I will do my best."

Twelve

It was no surprise that the Zambian team didn't start this morning, given the state of their feet and the fact they lost their shoes and running packs. That could have been us.

On Day 3, we're running cross-country, not following any path or road, but assuming the topo map is correct, the course I've laid out should be reasonably easy. And the route proves to be picturesque, too. Plus, we have it all to ourselves.

A brief flash of anxiety ripples through my gut as I remember how badly things went wrong for us in the Verde Island race when we deviated from the recommended course, but this is a completely different place and time. And presumably the Secret Service drone is up there somewhere, keeping an eye on us.

The landscape is sandy and mostly flat, dry grassland dotted with clumps of trees and bushes. I have no clue what most of the vegetation is, but nobody could miss the spectacular purple blooms of the jacaranda trees that dot this region. Birds chatter warnings as we jog under the branches, and up ahead beneath the biggest one, we see a big group of small pointy-nosed animals skitter from the tree's shade into the underbrush.

"Weasels?" Bash guesses.

"Mongooses," I tell him. "A business of mongooses."

"What?" Bash laughs. "Not a flock of mongeese?"

"Nope, a business. Or a mob or a pack." Once in a long while, I get to enjoy the fact that I know something from my zoo work that he doesn't. But it is weird how we have all these strange names for groups of animals. Why are some herds and some flocks and some packs? A murder of crows, a pod of orcas, a school of fish. Who comes up with all of this?

As we run, I study the pools of shade cast by each tree. I know lions like to hang out in such places, but I'm relieved that I don't see any big cats. A few miles further, we see a herd of goats and the young shepherd who is guarding them, so this must be a relatively safe area. The boy watches us curiously, his hands draped over a long stick balanced across his shoulders. He doesn't look any older than twelve, and his wary gaze reminds me of Aaron. Raising a hand, he waves shyly and calls out something in an African tongue. We shout "Hello!" and wave back.

We surprise two giraffes at a stream, their front feet spraddled out to the sides, their long necks stretched down as they drink. As we emerge from the woods, they lift their heads, snorting in surprise, then, in slow motion, they reposition themselves and lope away. I feel guilty that we scared them from the water, but I'm happy that we're making good time, and their presence means that there are probably no crocodiles lurking nearby. The stream proves to be less than a foot deep, and we easily splash through to the other side.

This is like jogging through a peaceful zoo, but I start to get paranoid because everything is happening too smoothly. When we pause for a drink and a few gulps of energy gel, I take more readings with the compass and map. We're right on course. The forest grows more dense, and the tree canopy overhead is mostly thick enough to hide us from our drone, which always feels like a victory to me. I decide to enjoy the day. Sometimes things have got to go well, don't they?

As I slow to a stroll in the shade, sucking on my water tube, I hear the sound of branches breaking. I scan the landscape to find the source. A flash of green motion in the distance draws my attention, and when the breaking branch is lowered, an elephant stands behind it. I point.

"It's amazing that this scrubby forest can actually hide an elephant," I tell Bash. "He's a lone male, probably a teenager that just got tossed out of the herd. Poor guy."

The crack of another breaking branch sounds from our other side. Bash turns to look. "This scrubby forest can hide two elephants." There's a brief pause, and then he adds, "Even a whole herd."

Crap, he's right. They're farther away, but sighting between the trees, I can see a huge elephant, probably the matriarch leader, and several others behind her. Even worse, they're spread out in a fan, and they're moving toward us.

I knew this day was going too well.

"This way." I walk toward the lone male.

"Uh, Tarzan," Bash says, "That way lies another elephant."

"You want to confront one young elephant, or a whole herd?"

He falls in beside me, but nervously asks, "Is there a no-elephant option?"

"Not unless we want to lose miles and time." I maintain my determined march, keeping a wary eye on the young male, who spots us and stands back from his meal, stiff-legged, ears spread out, eyes glued to the two human intruders. His rigid posture is not a good sign.

"Tana?" Bash murmurs.

"Don't worry," I tell him. I'm worried enough for the two of us. "I know elephants."

"Bailey is not a wild elephant," Bash reminds me.

"You keep an eye on the girls back there," I tilt my head in the direction of the approaching herd. "And I'll deal with this guy. If we have to."

"You'll *deal* with him?"

The young male flaps his ears and raises his trunk. Another not-good sign.

"Just walk quietly past," I tell Bash.

The teenage pachyderm rumbles and shifts anxiously from foot to foot. His tusks are small, but plenty big enough to kill us fragile homo sapiens. He trumpets. An elephant in the approaching herd answers back. My blood temperature drops twenty degrees at the thought that they might join forces.

We try to sneak past, a hundred feet away from this youngster, but he's feeling his territorial oats and decides to challenge, taking a step in our direction.

I put my hand on Bash's arm. "Stop."

"You sure about this?" His voice is higher than usual, but he halts and stands beside me and we both face the elephant.

I don't answer. I'm not sure about anything. I know what works with Bailey, but this isn't Bailey.

The young elephant flaps his ears, raises his trunk again, and takes two steps toward us. Bash tenses and sucks in a breath, but stays in place.

"Take two steps toward him, now," I command.

"Shit," Bash hisses as we advance two steps in unison.

The youngster stands his ground, tossing his head.

"One more," I tell my partner. Like soldiers on parade, we goose-step forward again.

After a couple of seconds more of the staring contest, the teenager whirls around and retreats, his feet raising red dust as he trots away.

On our other side, the herd is still coming our way. "Now, we run," I tell Bash.

And we take off, still more or less on the course I had plotted. "I'm so glad that worked out," Bash comments dryly.

Me too. I smile at him. I really had no idea what that elephant might do, but I know from experience that young males often try to bluff when they are unsure of their place in the animal hierarchy. It's the giant older bulls and the herd leaders—the matriarchs—that are ready to stomp you into a piece of bloody leather.

"Only about twenty kilometers to go," I tell Bash.

"Piece of cake." He speeds up, and I kick into higher gear to keep up with him. Now my mind is on cake. I hope there's some for dinner tonight.

After another kilometer, the forest grows thicker, so we must have run out of elephant territory. We need to watch carefully for animals among the trees, so we slow down a bit and scan ahead as far as we can, which is not far. We surprise a troop of baboons foraging on the ground. They rush up the nearby trees, screeching in alarm. Then we stumble across a beat-up Land Rover, which seems really out of place, because there are no roads or even trails anywhere close. A local farmer? Or maybe a lost tourist?

"Oh crap," Bash groans softly, pointing.

I follow his extended finger and it takes me a minute, but I finally spot two men in camouflage fatigues creeping through the brush a hundred yards ahead of the vehicle. They are both carrying ugly black rifles that resemble the semi-automatics soldiers carry in war movies. Beyond them, an animal is rooting around. When I squint to focus, that animal transforms itself into a rhinoceros.

A mother rhino, apparently, because there's a tiny pig-like creature staggering on the ground beside it, wet and shaky on its feet. The big rhino nudges the baby with the front of her horn.

It's pretty clear what's about to happen. That rhino mom is about to die at the hands of those two poachers.

Thirteen

I frantically search the shrubbery, the ground, for any kind of a weapon, and I finally spy a fist-sized rock in the red dirt about a yard away. I snatch it up and turn in the direction of the poachers.

"No," Bash warns.

I have terrible aim, I know that. So as I let it fly, I'm praying that this rock will connect with any part of one of these poachers. Head, shoulders, back, I don't care, as long as it stops them.

The rock smacks into a tree to the right of the two men with a solid *thwock*. Dry leaves shower down on their heads.

As the two men swivel around, Bash tackles me, dragging me to the ground, his eyes wild.

Crashing noises head toward us.

"We've got to run," Bash says, stating the obvious.

And then we take off, back the way we came. A shot rings out and I fear the baby rhino has just become an orphan, but then Bash stumbles and grabs his right forearm, swearing.

"Bash!"

"Keep going!"

I glance over my shoulder and see the poachers running after us, their rifles aimed in our direction.

"Zag!" I bark as another shot rings out.

And we begin to zig and zag separately, leaping over bushes and dodging trees. Several more gunshots zing through the air, and I can't help yelping as a lightning bolt blazes a burning trail across my left shoulder. But I keep running.

Soon we're leaving the poachers behind. But then I hear the engine of their Land Rover cough to life. As the growl of the vehicle grows louder and closer, I have an abrupt flashback to the night the ninjas chased me after murdering my parents. Terror washes over me in a dark wave.

Shake it off, shake it off. I focus on the terrain ahead of me and on keeping sight of Bash as I zig and zag among the trees.

Another hundred yards and Bash waves to me to duck behind some bushes. We crouch down, breathing hard. Bash's right forearm is bleeding trails of red that streak down his wrist and cover his hand like a bad tattoo of a tentacled creature. I have new body work, too, rivulets of blood dribbling front and back from a stinging slash across the top of my left shoulder. With all the adrenalin in my system, the pain is not too bad right now. That will probably change. It's a damn good thing these guys are lousy shots.

The engine noise roars closer. I motion for us to crawl into the thicket we're squatting beside, and on our hands and knees, we burrow our way deep into the thorny brush. The scratching of the sharp spikes hurts like hell on our bare arms and faces, but hiding seems like our best bet right now.

The Land Rover stops somewhere close. I clap a hand over my mouth, afraid that the poachers will hear my hoarse breathing.

A snapping noise draws our attention to the left. A branch breaks and swishes through the air as an elephant stuffs it into its mouth. His eyes round, Bash points, like I wouldn't notice a large pachyderm mowing down the vegetation only a few yards away.

It's the young male that was trailing the herd. We've run right back to him.

The poachers' voices are close by, sounding urgent and excited at the same time. They've probably seen the elephant. His tusks are small, but ivory's still ivory.

Then I see the two men, or at least flashes of them through the intertwined branches. The elephant trumpets as he sees them.

I can't watch them shoot him. I can't watch him die. But I don't want to die, either. I'm on the verge of shutting my eyes when I spy the matriarch, ears flapping, her trunk held high in the air like a medieval battle standard. She crashes through the forest, a live locomotive that has jumped the track, her female army close behind. The two men turn in her direction, shout and start to raise their rifles. She's still barreling toward them and she folds her ears back and rolls her trunk. That's when I know she's not just threatening, she's out to kill. Before the two men can aim their weapons, the elephant herd is on top of them, their trunks roping around the poachers' arms and necks like demonic pythons, raking and stabbing the men with their tusks, stomping them with their massive feet. The violence is terrifying.

All the elephants trumpet nonstop. The poachers scream. The pandemonium is deafening, a thousand horns blasting at skull-shattering volume. Between the clouds of red dust all those elephant feet stir up and the thorny branches in front of our faces, it's hard to make out exactly what is happening, but I can discern human shapes from elephants. One man falls almost instantly. He stays down and is immediately surrounded by a circle of elephants.

The other tries to crawl away. The matriarch snags an ankle with her trunk, scoops him up with her tusks, and tosses him high into the air. When he lands, she rushes over to his limp form and jabs him, impaling him through the abdomen with a wet, sucking sound. She shakes the poacher's body off her tusks, then curls her trunk again, places her forehead against his body and almost does a headstand on top of him. I hear a couple of cracking noises I don't want to speculate on.

Abruptly, the attack is over. The trumpeting stops. The herd communicates only with rumbling noises. All the elephants, even the young male, take their time exploring the bodies of the men, touching the limp corpses with their trunks. The matriarch uses a forefoot to nudge the poacher her comrades killed, as if to assure herself that he's dead. The corpse is coated with blood and dirt and it flops in the dust like a rag doll, so there's no doubt. The herd investigates the rifles, too, scooting them over the ground with their tusks, stepping on them with their forefeet. I worry that an elephant may accidentally fire one of the weapons, but although there are several loud snaps as the weapons break, no bullets are unleashed.

They say that elephants have amazing memories. I suspect this herd has experienced poachers before.

The females group up, rumbling loudly, and now I see a couple of small calves that wisely stayed in the rear during the attack. The elephants rub flanks, touch each other with their trunks. Maybe it's the pachyderm version of high-fiving. When the young male tries to join in, he is shoved away, and the matriarch tosses her head and trumpets at him. He reluctantly moves off, his trunk hanging limp now. He looks sad and lonely. I want to go out there and comfort him like I would Bailey.

Bash nudges my good shoulder and with a lift of his chin, directs my attention back to the matriarch. She's staring in our direction, her trunk lifted like a teapot spout, her ears fanned out.

There's no doubt that she can smell us. She takes a step toward our hiding place. And then another, faster this time.

An alarm goes off in my head. My heart leaps into overdrive. I slap my hands onto the ground and turn to crawl out of the thorn bush.

Bash's fingers curl around my calf to stop me.

"I have to," I whisper. "Stay here."

Like a rioting street mob, these elephants are high on blood lust. I've seen what Bailey can do when he's in a temper; I ended up with him because the zoo was afraid he would eventually kill someone. Any of these pachyderms could easily plow through that thorn bush and stomp Bash and me like pumpkins.

Fourteen

When I scramble from the thicket on my hands and knees, the matriarch stops in her tracks. Her ears stand out at the sides of her head like sails. Behind her, the herd watches closely. If she gives the signal, they will be on me in seconds.

Slowly, rising only inches at a time, I stand up. Terrified does not begin to describe how scared I am right now. Minutes ago I was afraid *for* these elephants, now I am petrified *of* them.

The matriarch is a monster, towering far above me. She shakes her head. Dust flies from her skin, surrounding us both in a cloud of red powder. Making a huffing sound, she flaps her ears in warning. Her eyes never leave mine. She stretches her trunk out as far as it will go, testing the air. Taking in my scent.

I smell like sweat and fear and worst of all, like a human. Like those two men she just killed.

My heart might stop beating.

Looking directly at her, I murmur softly, "Hello, beautiful." And then I slowly raise my arms, inch by inch, my hands open, palms up to show I have no weapons.

She takes a few more steps toward me. One. Two. Three. A rush of blood drains from my head to my toes. My vision goes white and misty.

Now is not the time to faint. I take a deep breath and try to swallow, but my mouth is as dry as the Kalahari Desert.

Behind me, Bash gasps. "Tana!"

She takes another step. Now the matriarch is close enough to touch me with her outstretched trunk. I watch, mesmerized as her nostrils widen to sniff me, the tip of her trunk less than a foot from my chest.

Uber slowly, I extend a hand toward that trunk. The tips of my fingers meet the sensitive grasping end of her trunk. We both take one more step forward, our eyes locked on each other. I stand immobile as she explores my body, moving the tip of her trunk over my head, snarling my hair, and then sliding her trunk along my torso and arms. I'm used to being slimed by Bailey's greetings; the tickle of elephant exploration is not new to me. Her trunk lingers over my bleeding shoulder, and then wipes wet blood down my bicep. Her touch is amazingly gentle.

What can this elephant be thinking? Did she witness the poachers chasing us? Does she feel sorry for me? Or is she about to wrap her trunk around my neck and slam me to the ground? While I believe that being crushed by a wild elephant would be a more noble death than being shot by a poacher, I'd rather not die at all today.

Then the matriarch backs up a step, flaps her ears once, and pivots on her back feet, turning in place. Dismissing us, she strolls regally away. The herd follows her and they vanish through the forest. Only the young male is left.

As my partner crawls out of the thicket, the teenage elephant jerks his head up and down and raises his trunk and trumpets as if to brag that he could still be a threat.

Bash glares at him. "Oh, please. Don't be ridiculous."

The juvenile male actually backs up a step.

Bash yanks a thorn out of his hair and then rubs his head. "That was absolutely terrifying, but also absolutely astounding."

I can finally breathe again, and I curl my lips into a trembling smile. "It was, wasn't it?"

We break into our first aid kits and paste adhesive bandages over our wounds. I'm relieved to see that the blood on Bash's forearm is oozing from a graze like my shoulder slash, not from an entry wound.

We retrace our steps through the forest, stopping to glance at the corpses of the poachers. Their bodies are so misshapen that it's hard to tell they were human beings only minutes ago. The killings were a horrific thing to watch, but I can't help feeling that this is a brutal form of justice: these men lived by killing, and then died by being killed.

That dark thought leads me directly to my own dilemma. If I ever figure out who my parents' murderers are, will I want to kill them? I want to *erase* them from the planet, but I can't actually imagine myself taking someone's life. I usually carry spiders out of my house instead of flattening them.

When Bash and I continue on our original path, we discover that the poachers' Land Rover has been overturned, dented and punctured. I guess at least one elephant was busy taking care of equipment while the others dealt with the armed men.

Team Eight warms up to a trot, and finally to our usual lope. As we pass the spot where the poachers were originally parked, we glance off to the small clearing. The mama rhino is still there, and her goofy looking lump of a newborn is suckling under her armored belly.

A little more than an hour later, we stumble into camp. Our drone catches up with us after we leave the forest and follows, filming us as we again race the Ethiopian team. They beat us by less than a hundred yards to end up in third place behind—of course—Marco Senai and his partner. The Zimbabwean team is first again. We are fourth.

The medic staffing the first aid tent exclaims over our bullet grazes and thorn scratches as he applies GluSkin and fresh adhesive patches. When we explain about the poachers, all the Zimbabwean officials' reactions seem almost nonchalant, like this happens every day.

Maybe it does. That possibility is horrible to think about. I'm glad the elephants were victorious today.

"Did you see the animal these poachers were hunting?" one of the race officials asks me, his expression eager.

I shake my head, and then Bash takes the cue and copies my motion. I don't feel safe telling the Zimbabweans about the rhinos. Who knows where poachers get their information? I don't tell them about the elephants killing those men, either. When someone stumbles across that scene, the reason for the poachers' demise will be obvious.

Seven teams started this morning. On the second day, the team from Botswana and the pair from Egypt dropped out due to injuries. This morning, the Zambians. Dinner (with coconut cake this time) comes and goes with only two more teams—the Germans and the South African team—coming in. Dante Green is thrilled that his team has climbed to third place, and he spends most of dinner telling the rest of us how Team Nine will beat everyone else tomorrow. Even his partner Sarah seems irritated by him.

The vids are almost non-existent tonight, probably because the television van isn't here. Just a few unimaginative clips of all the teams taken from overhead. I notice the Germans run past two ostriches, and I'm jealous of that. When I mention the giant birds, Danai from Team One informs the table that there is a tribe in Zimbabwe called the Ostrich People because they have only two toes on their feet. I'm not sure whether to believe her, but her teammate Rudo confirms the tale. Ugh. Poor people.

My shoulder hurts, and I'm glad this third camp is another series of tent cabins with cots instead of hammocks. No internet, though, which is just as well. I don't have the energy to deal with any worrisome news from home or any more cryptic messages from P.A. Patterson.

Bash and I offer our Secret Squirrels cans of beer, which to our surprise, Pratt and Lyman gratefully accept, tucking them away and saying they will enjoy them in their tent later. Apparently they are human after all. Seems like everyone except for Dante is loosening up.

Gretchen Vogel and Janelle Hurst are the only pale faces

in camp tonight, and I quickly give up watching for the Mom Lookalike. By sunset, the racers from Swaziland still haven't arrived. I can't remember their names, but I can picture both of them, lean and fierce-looking, a brother and sister in their teens. Although I'm pretty sure they both understood English, they refused to speak anything but their native language, so nobody here has talked with them.

"The fellow was limping a bit when they set off this morning," Janelle tells me, shaking her head.

The official rescue team goes out with searchlights mounted on their Land Rover to look for the missing racers. As Bash and I stand outside and stare at the stars, saying goodnight to the world before we retire to our tents, lions roar back and forth, claiming their territories not too far away in the bush.

I think about that newborn rhino we saw today and worry about all the gentle soft creatures out there among all the teeth and claws and bullets.

Fifteen

On the final day of the race, we wake up to low clouds and the news that the team from Swaziland was eventually found in a tree surrounded by Cape buffalo. The racers are fine, but because they didn't make it to the checkpoint by dark, they're out.

A smoky flavor taints the air again this morning; the atmosphere seems thick enough to eat with a spoon. Bash and I add bandannas to our race uniforms, knotting them around our necks in case we need them as face masks. The smoke is from more field clearing, we're told, just small contained blazes, nothing to worry about. The facial expressions of most of the teams around the breakfast table are glum. I can tell that none of us is looking forward to filling our lungs with all the particulate matter in the air, but at least we are all equally challenged that way. Except perhaps for the Zimbabwean pair, who seem not at all concerned. Maybe they know we will soon run out of the smoke zone.

Rudo and Danai on Team One are also the only competitors who do not have a single scratch or bruise visible on their perfect complexions. The rest of us are covered with scratches and bruises and bandages, making us look like boxers who lost our matches. Bash and I are wearing the same clothes from yesterday, so we are decorated with splotches of dried blood, too.

Our drone lifts off behind us as we dash into the hazy forest surrounding the camp. The recommended route is to follow a bunch of these small intersecting roads, but that would add miles. The course I've charted for today is partially along a dirt track that passes for a regional road here. Then we'll take a shortcut through the bush, which is the longest straight stretch we plan to run, and then we'll meet up with another vehicle track that should take us right to the finish line.

Bash and I are excellent cross-country runners, and if we don't encounter trouble—always a big "if" in these races—we should move substantially ahead, and maybe even win. I will try to make up for all the time and mental energy I've wasted thinking about my relatives, and do my best in this final stretch. I owe that to Bash and to Kent and Clark at Dark Horse Networks.

The smoke lies low, snaking between trees and making it hard to see for more than a few yards, and I worry that we might literally run into that elephant herd or a pride of lions before we are aware they're close by. Then again, those animals are probably smart enough to move to a clear area. But the haze would make perfect cover for a pack of thugs, and humans are the animals treacherous enough to think that way. We wet our bandannas with water from the hydration packs on our backs and trot as fast as we can without coughing, but the smoke stings our eyes. Tears stream down our cheeks. The air temperature is variable, but in places it feels as hot as an oven in preheat mode. The situation is nerve-wracking, not to mention supremely irritating. This would never be allowed in a race in any civilized country. I have to keep pulling out the compass to be sure we're still on course.

After about ninety minutes of this aggravation, the wind picks up and the air seems to clear a bit, so we increase our pace. We are running well when we hear crashing in the brush ahead of us. We stop, holding our breath as we listen. Please, not another herd of elephants. Whatever is making all the snapping and cracking sounds, it sounds big, and it's moving our way fast.

A herd of impala burst out of the trees. A calf nearly collides with Bash, darting awkwardly to the side at the last second. The antelope race past us, not in the least interested in our presence, which makes me think that they're being pursued by something else. And then, sure enough, a few seconds after the last antelope passes, a hyena shoots out of the gray smog.

My pulse hiccups at the sight of that predator, but the hyena barely glances at us before it runs on. Bash and I pause to sip some water, pushing our drinking tubes up under our bandannas as we nervously study our surroundings.

"Only one?" Bash finally says. It seems strange to hear my partner talk without being able to see his lips move.

"Guess so. That seems really weird. I didn't know hyenas hunted; I thought they were mainly scavengers." But then again, I only know caged hyenas, and we don't allow any predators to kill their meals in the zoo where I work. That tends to upset visitors.

The wind gusts from a new direction, hot as a hair dryer. I suddenly have a really bad feeling about that. "Bash, I..."

Then, with a whoosh that threatens to suck the air from our lungs, a scrawny tree in front of us bursts into flames like an exploding rocket.

"Shit!" Bash exclaims.

The flames fan out sideways to the surrounding trees like the act was choreographed, igniting a wall of fire. We turn in place, looking for an escape route. The trees that we just ran through are not on fire, but they soon will be, because beyond them, orange tongues of flames reach into the sky.

"Oh...my...God, Bash." It's not a wall of fire, it's a circle. The oven in which we stand has just switched from pre-heat to broil.

Sixteen

"Tana." Bash reaches out his hand to take mine. A last gallant gesture?

We stare at each other, our eyes wide over our kerchiefs, sweat drenching our faces. I have a fleeting thought of kissing him before we are engulfed in flames.

"We have to run." I can barely choke out the words.

"Which direction?" Bash finishes with a hacking cough.

I look up, for some inane reason hoping that our Secret Squirrels could save us with their drone. Nothing but thick gray smoke overhead. No drone could find us in this dense haze. If this was a more sophisticated race, we'd be wearing GPS trackers.

With every passing second, the flames dance closer. Which direction? If only we had a birds-eye view of this disaster, maybe we'd have a chance. But now, as the flames and smoke close in, I can barely see my race partner right beside me.

Then, amid the crackling flames, I hear a distant high trumpeting call. Then another. I turn in that direction. I feel more than hear a low rumbling through the earth. I tug on my partner's hand. "This way, Bash."

Through my streaming eyes, I can see nothing but fire and smoke in that direction, but I pull harder. "I hear elephants."

All he says is, "Lead the way."

"Run like your life depends on it." I intertwine the fingers of my right hand with those of his left. "Don't let go."

Hand in hand, we dash straight toward the flames. It's absolutely terrifying, but I'd rather burn while running than stand still and let the fire reduce me to ashes.

The smoke is so dense that we can't see what's ahead until we are upon it: a flaming bush, a smoldering log. We leap over charred debris, flames searing our skin. I'm surprised to see that not everything is blazing, but the landscape is all black, gray, red, yellow, and it's all scorching hot.

Sparks burn holes in my tights, shirt, and baseball cap—it feels like a hundred hornets stinging all at once. My eyes are so tear-filled that I can barely see even in the few clearings where the burning has completely stopped. The soles of my feet feel like they could combust at any second. Are my hi-tech running shoes melting into my flesh? Worst of all, my lungs feel like they will soon stop working. I know Bash is feeling all this, too. But we keep running through the nightmare.

I hear another trumpet ahead. I pull Bash toward it. A branch crashes down only inches behind us. The elephants don't sound as if they are being cooked, but then I've never heard elephants dying before. At least, if they're dying, Team Eight will die with them, and there's no creature on earth I'd rather share a grave with.

But I keep running. And coughing. And crying. I can't die here. And I can't die now.

If I'm not around, what will happen to Bailey? If I die, odds are that my ornery elephant will be killed. And who would take on a disturbed, violent boy like Aaron?

The ground beneath our feet is uneven, and we stumble as we race through the burn. My eyes are streaming with sweat and searing smoke. Bash goes down on one knee, I tug him back up. Then I trip and end up on my hands and knees, coughing so hard I can't push myself back up to my feet.

No! I can't die now.

Thank God my partner stops and jerks me up. He's coughing so hard he can barely move. My insides are burning from the acrid smoke—my nostrils, my throat, my lungs. My skin hurts, and I expect it to bubble up like bacon any second now. Bash has to be in the same shape. We make it only few more yards and then we both fall simultaneously, ending up sprawled across the ground.

Oh God. Is this it?

Bailey! Aaron!

Is that mud I feel under my fingers? I curl them and crawl ahead. Blessedly cool water kisses my chest, then my knees, the backs of my burning hands. Bash and I scuttle like monitor lizards to the middle of a stream. It's deep enough that when we sit on our backsides, it laps at our necks. I want to shout hurrah, but I'm gagging and gasping so hard that I can't utter another sound. My partner is in the same condition.

Flames line the borders of the creek or river or whatever this is, but the stream here is at least thirty feet wide from bank to bank. It looks like we won't burn to death. It seems more likely the smoke inhalation will do us in.

Bash ducks his head under the water, and I follow suit, coming up with my bandanna soaked and harder to breathe through, but the moist air is somewhat comforting. Between coughing fits, I poke my water tube beneath my bandanna and suck in a mouthful of liquid. The water from my pack is hot, but it relieves my scorched mouth and throat. Our hands find each other again, and I can see Bash's green eyes shining above his kerchief.

We may survive after all.

The wind gusts, and as the dense smoke separates into fingers, we discover that we are not alone. Less than seventy feet away is a gigantic dark mass, and as my eyes clear, it morphs into an elephant. Then, as the fire burns out on the north side of the stream, the smoke thins and we can see that multiple elephants stand in the middle of the stream. The older ones fill their trunks with water and spray the babies before they shower themselves. I feel their rumbling through my own belly as they communicate with each other.

The air continues to clear as the fire moves farther away, and Bash and I can actually breathe for a few minutes before the next coughing jag. The closest elephant turns its head toward us. It's the matriarch we encountered the day before yesterday. I feel like kissing her because her herd's trumpeting led us in this direction. The matriarch, however, may want to kill us. The brutal deaths of the poachers replay themselves in my head—was that only yesterday? And now her herd has just been tortured in a conflagration—does she understand that the fire was caused by humans?

Whether or not she associates people with the fire, this elephant knows that humans are not her friends, and she has her whole defensive squad with her.

"Just sit, Bash." I tell him. "Don't move."

He makes a snorting sound which turns into a hacking cough, and then he pulls his kerchief down around his neck. "If they move"—he inclines his head toward the river bank—"I'm moving."

I take my eyes off the matriarch for a second to focus on what he's indicating. The river bank dips into a couple of wallows along the shore, and there's a fair-sized crocodile in each one. Then, in the closest pool, the surface of the water undulates. Make that two crocodiles in that pool, a lone croc in the other. And unbelievably, a massive lump at the edge of the stream raises its head and morphs into a male lion. He's completely soaked. Clods of mud matt his mane. Dirty water drips from his snout.

We are surrounded. While I'm happy all these creatures lived through the fire, Bash and I may have survived the flames only to be stomped or devoured.

My gasping and hacking is nearly under control, and the sky is clearing as I turn my attention back to the matriarch elephant. She's not focused on us, though. Her eyes are fixed on the lion. She rumbles low in her belly, which apparently is a signal, because the other elephants move closer to her. Then she raises her ears and her trunk, blasts out an ear-shattering trumpet, and takes a step toward the lion.

As he reluctantly hauls his rear quarters out of the water, I see large clumps of fur have been burned from his hide, leaving wounds as red as raw meat. He's in no shape for confrontation, and with a weary glance over his shoulder, he pads silently into the blackened forest and vanishes into the ashes.

Several of the elephants trumpet and then rumble as they cluster closer together. Celebrating their survival? Talking about where to go next? People think I'm some sort of elephant whisperer because I have Bailey, but most of the time I don't have a clue what his vocalizations mean. Gestures are our only common language. So it is with relief that I watch the matriarch lead her group away into the burned area behind the lion.

Finally Bash and I feel safe enough to stand. We laugh, high-five, and he chortles in a hoarse voice, "We are *alive*, Tana!"

Then he leans over and kisses me. I throw my arms around his neck and kiss him back, celebrating. We are alive.

Bash has a blister on his cheek, and several more on his arms and legs, and his hair is uneven where it has been charred. My skin feels sunburned. I feel a deeper burn on my neck, and I see blisters on my arms and legs, too. Holes dot our clothes and our packs. One of Bash's pack straps is nearly burnt through, so we fix it with two carabiners and a piece of cord.

But amazingly, neither of us suffered major damage.

"God bless those elephants," Bash says.

"Yes." God-or-whoever-is-out-there that watches over living creatures. With my history, it's a little difficult to believe in a benevolent overlord in the heavens who plans everything. The animals that found the river survived, but how many others burned to death? And why did they have to die?

I still don't have a why for the murders of my parents, and I can't believe their deaths are part of some grand plan to make the world a better place.

"Run?" Bash suggests.

Seventeen

I pull out my compass. There's a little water inside the plastic casing, but it still works. The map is a sodden wad of paper, but I think I remember the major landmarks. "That way." I point, and we take off, our shoes squishing as we slog up the river bank.

The crocs don't move, making me wonder if smoke has the same paralyzing effect on reptiles as it does on bees. I'll have to ask the reptile keepers at the zoo.

"Miles to go?" Bash asks as we enter the burned-out woods. His voice is hoarse, and he finishes with a cough.

My voice sounds equally rough. "It was about eighteen kilometers when I last checked." And then I cough, too, which hurts my throat. I swish lukewarm water from my drinking tube through my mouth before I swallow it. The liquid soothes the rawness there a tiny bit, but as I breathe through my nose, I find my sinuses hurt almost as much.

My shoes feel like they no longer fit right, especially the left one, but I've got no choice but to run in them. I try to ignore the ache in my left foot and keep my strides even and steady so I don't throw out a knee or hip joint. All the little burned spots are making their presence known, too, especially now that salty sweat is oozing into them; it feels like I'm being tortured with the burning ends of cigarettes. The bullet graze on my shoulder chimes in with a background ache.

Bash's clenched jaw and the frown lines on his forehead tell me my partner is experiencing similar sensations.

I remind myself that I am lucky to be alive, and that it's the last day of the race. *Pain is temporary. Suck it up, Tana.* There will be good food and first aid at the finish line, and maybe even whawha. I can rest on the long plane ride back home. Bailey and Aaron and Sabrina will happily greet me when I arrive at WildRun. Emilio will visit when he can, and one of these days, we *will* go see those monarchs.

I conjure my family's happy faces into my imagination to take my mind off my pain. Is it weird that I always envision my elephant first?

Our feet stir up clouds of ashes and the air is still hazy with smoke, making us stop periodically to hack up clots of black phlegm. Dark snot oozes out of our nostrils, so we keep our bandannas loosely tied around our necks so we can just pull them up as needed. Run, cough, spit, wipe. It becomes a disgusting regular routine that continues for over an hour. But then we burst out of the forest and onto the road I had hoped to find after our shortcut through the bush. At least I hope it's the road I saw on the map.

We continue to trot along the road and soon come to an intersecting track, and for a few seconds, I rejoice inwardly that we are miraculously on course. The path I plotted—was that only last night?—follows rural roads for the last part of the race. We should be about two hours from the final checkpoint.

My left foot is killing me, and my right is only marginally better. I have to think of something else. I wonder where the elephants went, and if wildlife can stay hidden from poachers now that so much of the bush has burned. Did the other competitors get caught up in the fire? Have they already crossed the finish line? All miserable thoughts.

I turn my head to study my race partner beside me, because, well, misery loves company.

"We're alive, Tana," Bash says through clenched teeth. "And the race is almost done."

A buzz makes us glance up. A drone streaks by overhead. It returns, hovers for a second, and then rises higher. After another couple of minutes, we hear a vehicle approach behind us. A Land Rover covered in camouflage paint soon roars up. Pratt is focused on driving because the track we're on is full of rocks and holes, but Lyman's eyes rake over Team Eight, scrutinizing our bodies and clothes through dark sunglasses. After a few seconds of this inspection, Bash flicks his hand in their direction and then points straight ahead.

Pratt gives him a little salute, and then the Land Rover zips off up the road, leaving us choking in a cloud of red dust. Doesn't the Secret Service realize that dust and car exhaust do not benefit The President's Son, especially after inhaling all that smoke?

We pick up the pace, and soon the signs and crowds at the finish line come into view. There's a big screen set up and cameras are tracking the racers as they come in. Team Eight is live on the screen. I glance down at my racing tee. Although there are a few holes in the fabric and one shoulder is stained with blood, the Dark Horse Networks logo is still intact. As we cross the finish line, I thrust out my chest so the logo will show in the photo.

Pratt and Lyman are in the crowd and clap for us along with the others. Team One, the Zimbabweans, are here, clean, combed, and camera-ready. As soon as we're over the line, I drop to the ground and yank off my pack and running shoes. Bash does the same.

After a few minutes of our typical gasping and rolling on the ground, Marco Senai and his partner Hasina Okeke of Team Three emerge from the group of spectators to congratulate us. They are also dressed in clean clothes, telling me they've been here for at least ten minutes.

After observing my burned clothes and hair, Marco comments, "I see that Team Eight has taken a shortcut."

"I don't recommend it," I tell him.

"We were only a bit ahead of the conflagration."

"Did you win?" I ask hopefully, looking up at Marco from my position on the ground. My throat is still burning, and I feel nauseous.

His lips twitch as if he's not sure what to say.

Hasina tells us, "We are second."

"And the rest of the group?" Bash pushes himself to his feet. We are pretty sure after our fire escapade that we will finish close to the last of the pack.

"They are not yet here." Marco reaches out a hand and pulls me to my feet.

Team Eight came in third? Unbelievable.

I wish it could have been first for Bash and Clark and Kent but I'm more than pleased with third place. And with our survival.

Hasina collects my shoes and hands them to me. The soles of my shoes are melted into strange amoeba shapes; no wonder my feet are so bruised. I toss them into a trash can on my way to the dressing rooms.

Everyone back-slaps the Zimbabwean team, congratulating them on their win. Two more teams come in, first Team Five, Janelle Hurst and Andre Govender from South Africa, and then Dante Green and Sarah Bekele, Team Nine. Both teams complain about having to run extra miles because of a major bush fire.

It's not sportspersonlike, I know, but I'm pleased that the Real African-Americans came in two places behind Bash and me.

We stop by the first aid tent to get burn ointment. They have one tube, so we'll have to share.

"You are limping," the attendant observes as she hands the tube to me.

Duh. "Don't worry about it," I tell her.

The bags we packed for the finish are handed to us, and Bash and I are pointed to the showers.

"Fifteen minutes to the award ceremony," a woman in a race tee tells us. I'm not sure why she's wearing a whistle around her neck, like a track coach. She hands us each a plastic bottle of mango juice.

Where's the whawha? I want to whine, but I slug down

the juice as I dutifully limp toward the showers. There, I gratefully sluice off the dirt and smoke, finding double the number of burned spots on my skin than I noticed at first. The soles of my feet are painfully tender, but I'm happy that there are no burn blisters or bleeding wounds. My nostrils feel like they've been turned inside out. I try to inhale some water to rinse them, but that just makes me cough. The end of my ponytail is a charcoaled mess; it stinks to high heaven. I do my best to slather it with scented shampoo and conditioner and rake away the black bits with fingers and comb, but the strands are burned to different lengths. I know it will look like hell when it dries, so I pull it all back in a French braid and hope the newly shortened frizzles will stay there.

I dab ointment on the burn spots I can reach, and then I pull on a brand new, bright green Dark Horse Networks tee and black shorts. I swipe a lipstick across my mouth, slap a clean adhesive patch over my bullet graze, and that's as good as it's going to get. Strapping on my sandals hurts more than remaining barefoot, but I decide I should wear shoes to the award ceremony out of respect. This contest could use a dash of dignity.

When I emerge from the shower tent, Bash is waiting for me outside, his dark hair slicked back, the blister on his cheek deflated, a white bandage on his right forearm. He's wearing a new shirt dotted with the dozens of logos of his sponsors.

I help him spread ointment onto his cheek and then dot some on red spots that freckle his arms and legs.

Lyman slips out of the crowd to escort us to the bleachers where the winners will be announced and the awards given.

"Where's Pratt?" Bash asks.

"Sharing our drone footage." Lyman points toward the television van with his chin. Then he looks at Bash. "The drone lost you in the smoke for more than three hours."

Damn. So there will be no footage of the elephants that saved us, or the lion or crocs we shared our river refuge with. That would have been so sweet to see.

Lyman adds, "I can't tell you how relieved we were to find you after that fire."

"Not as relieved as we were to survive," Bash replies.

The final team, the Germans, come in, but nobody seems to care. I feel sorry for Gretchen and Walter Vogel. The two of them and the South Africans stick around for the awards ceremony. I also see Sarah Bekele in the crowd, but Dante Green is not present. He's probably off sulking somewhere. At least he's consistent.

At the side of the field, a knot of men are huddled and stacks of bills are changing hands. I hope that most of those betters made money with their wagers.

The organizers tell us to position ourselves on the bleachers as they announce the winners, the Zimbabweans on top, the Kenyans on the second level, and Bash and I on the third step down. Cameras roll as the winners receive ribbons around our necks, and we view the award ceremony on the big screen, our present selves intercut with scenes from the four days of the race.

"First place, the champions of the Extreme Africa Endurance Challenge..." The emcee draws out the announcement and I almost expect a drum roll before he finishes, "Team One, Rudo Musinga and Danai Mhere...from Zimbabwe! Our Zimbabwean Champions!"

The modelesque pair beams as they graciously bend down to allow a small boy and girl to place beribboned medals around their necks. The emcee repeats the announcement in Shona, and the crowd roars and continues to applaud as Team One climbs to the top tier of the bleachers. Danai and Rudo grasp their hands together and hold them up for the camera as more translations follow over the loudspeakers.

This scene plays out on the big screen, and then cuts to several shots of Team One running in various scenic locales. And then, as the emcee begins, "Second place—", a slice of footage fills the screen and leaves us all speechless.

The footage, clearly from a drone filming downward, shows a black van rolling up to the edge of a parking lot and stopping. Off to the side, the bleachers and television van and a flash of the finish line yellow tape can be seen through a scattering of trees that divides the area we are now in from that parking lot. The driver emerges and after a quick glance around, he slides open the side door of the van, and out hop Rudo Musinga and Danai Mhere. They dash off into the woods and vanish from the screen.

Less than a minute later, the film shows them trotting down the road toward the finish line.

Eighteen

The crowd goes silent for a few seconds. On the stand, Rudo and Danai shift their gaze from the screen and stare straight out over the heads of the crowd. Then the shouting begins, starting in the television van. I dart a glance at Lyman, who stands beside us at the bottom of bleachers. He grins and shrugs. Pratt soon joins him, striding over from the television van. His expression is uncharacteristically flustered as he buttons a USB drive into his chest pocket, but then he grins at Lyman and they high-five before Pratt slides on his sunglasses and becomes a Secret Service agent again.

Well, well. Our guards are good guys. Our suspicions about Team One are confirmed. The betting men hurriedly cram their winnings into their pockets as loud arguments break out, involving a lot of fingers poking into chests and raised fists.

There's widespread cacophony in multiple languages for a few seconds, and then an ear-splitting whistle brings all the noise to an abrupt halt. The woman with the whistle lowers it from the microphone, and then the emcee returns the microphone to his lips. Now he is flanked by two of the Zimbabwean soldiers, and another pair stands behinds him.

The emcee licks his lips and begins again. "In second place we have Team Three, Marco Senai and Hasina Okeke, from Kenya."

The crowd claps politely. Marco bows his head for the boy to place his second place medal around his neck. As his head comes up, I catch his eye and give him a two hands raised, WTF gesture. He merely shrugs and smiles. As he and Hasina pass by, he murmurs in his melodic tone, "It is Zimbabwe."

They climb the steps and take their places on the second tier.

Unbelievable. The organizers and seemingly, the crowd too, choose to pretend they didn't just see the proof that the Zimbabweans cheated, that the Kenyans are the actual champions. On the big screen, choppy film footage shows Marco and Hasina gracefully leaping over streams and trotting along a game path that cleaves a herd of zebra. The animals wheel at the sight of runners and dash away, creating a pretty scene for the drone camera.

Damn. They saw zebras? I wish we'd taken that route. I remember hearing zebras one evening, but we never saw any of those magnificent beasts. And someone else saw ostriches. I wish I'd seen those, too.

"In third place, The President's Son, Sebastian Callendro, and Tanzania Grey, from the United States of America."

I am still steamed as we take our places, but I try to plaster a happy expression on my face for my sponsors. Clark and Kent Nilsen will be pleased that I have made it to the winner circle wearing their company logo on my chest. Our film footage is sparse, showing Team Eight clean and rested-looking as we begin the race, and then our last two finishes, where Bash and I stagger into camp, looking as if we've been dragged fifty miles behind a truck. Apparently Zimbabwean television elected not to show the farmer that shot down the original drone, or perhaps the camera was too damaged by the crash.

I have mixed feelings about not seeing the elephant killings of the poachers, though. I sort of wish that brutal episode of justice had been recorded. Then again, for all I know, that might have caused the government here to execute the matriarch's herd for being confirmed people-killers.

The emcee concludes with major congratulations to all who worked on the race to move it to this glorious conclusion that should make the whole country proud. Of course there's no mention of racers cheating or getting lost or robbers lying in wait or field-clearing fires roaring out of control. While we wait to be released, I study the faces of the crowd. Some nod in agreement or support of the speaker, some are watching the beautiful scenes of Zimbabwe that now fill the screen, and a few are focused on the six of us standing on the bleachers.

As the announcements continue to repeat in multiple languages, I scan the crowd for a chestnut-haired white woman. Nobody even comes close to a Mom Lookalike, and my hopes finally flop all the way to the ground.

Finding my mother here was a ridiculous dream.

And I don't understand why P.A. Patterson sent me the invitation and that *See you soon* note if he didn't plan to show up.

Then a chilling thought hits me. Could one of the men watching us now be Patterson? If he meant to do me harm, he might not identify himself before he attacked.

Nineteen

After the award ceremony, we are told that within one hour, we must make our own way the short distance to the nearby airstrip for a short plane ride back to race camp in Victoria Falls, where the Extreme Africa Endurance Race will conclude with a party and banquet tonight for all involved. Then competitors will receive complimentary meals tomorrow as well as a night in our dormitory, followed by rides to the airport the day after.

It's unbelievable how precious the gifts of food and drink are after these races. Not to mention sleep, glorious sleep. Bash and I can barely put one foot in front of the other; we're too exhausted to even talk. I have no idea if The President's Son is happy or disappointed about coming in third.

Many of the competitors have friends and family at the finish line, so they are swallowed up by their fans. Team Eight has only our two Secret Squirrels in attendance. I keep studying everyone around us, expecting someone to approach, but nobody else does. Bash and I start the walk down the long mowed grass strip that leads to the airstrip. Our muscles are already getting stiff; we need to stay in motion. Pratt and Lyman follow at a distance, keeping a close eye on us.

No matter whether I win, finish in the top three, or don't make it that far, my emotions are always confused at the end of a race. I feel both gratitude and regret for the end of the contest. Right now, my whole body hurts; the tiny burns all over feel like they are still on fire. My feet ache and I take off my sandals to walk barefoot in the cool grass. The bullet graze on my shoulder stings.

But my brain feels numb. The poachers, the robbers, and the fire were all so horrific.

"I still can't believe it," Bash murmurs, shaking his head. "The cheating. The fix." He's referring to the Zimbabwean team.

"Yeah."

"Those elephants killing the poachers. Being held at gunpoint by those robbers. The fire."

So he's also thinking about all the bad things that are running through my brain.

"Yeah," I say again.

"This is Zimbabwe." His naturally deep voice slides into a perfect imitation of Marco Senai's Kenyan accent, which makes us both laugh.

"At least we saw Guinea fowl, bee-eaters, warthogs, antelope, giraffes, baboons, and crocodiles. And that newborn rhino!"

A smile slowly leaks onto his face. "You faced down wild elephants."

"I did." My colleagues at the zoo will be impressed.

"And I got to race with you one more time."

"I am honored once again, Your Royal Highness." I hold out my juice bottle, and he taps his against it in a toasting gesture. Tapping plastic together is not nearly as satisfactory as clinking wine glasses or beer mugs, but we finish off by raising our bottles high and gulping down big mouthfuls anyway.

As I swallow, I'm thinking about how I didn't find that chestnut-haired woman or meet the mysterious P.A. Patterson. A rustling in the bushes to my side startles me, and I step sideways, crashing into Bash.

Our guards go on full alert, their hands under their shirttails, pulling out their weapons.

I expect a gazelle or a monkey or a reporter, but out steps a woman dressed in khaki pants and shirt. A floppy hat hides her hair and sunglasses obscure most of her face. With a strangely dramatic flourish, she pulls off the hat and shakes down shoulder-length chestnut hair. Then she removes her sunglasses.

Mom! The word doesn't escape my lips, but my heart sings it loud and clear.

Her eyes go wide as she takes in the guns behind us. She reaches for me, but Pratt and Lyman grab her, drag her away, twisting her arms behind her back, yelling, "Back off, back off, down on your knees!"

I bellow at the Secret Squirrels. "*You* guys back off!"

They don't move until Bash takes Pratt's arm and tells him to give us some space. They reluctantly release my mother, but pat her down before they retreat with Bash to a space about thirty feet away, keeping a close watch on me and the stranger.

Mom! I throw myself into her arms. Over her shoulder I see the perplexed looks on the faces of Pratt and Lyman as they watch.

Her hug feels so right, so much like home. I blather like a sloppy drunk, sobbing into her hair. "Mom, Mom, Mom. I can't believe it's you. I thought you were dead."

In my head, joy and rage battle for control of my emotions. Mom's alive! How could she do this to me and Aaron? "Mom, what happened? Why are you here? Why did you leave me alone all these years? Where's Dad?"

I can't make my arms let go of her. Her shoulders are heaving under my grip, and I realize she's crying, too, so hard she's not answering any of my questions.

"Mom? You don't have to answer. I don't care; I love you. I can't believe you're here. That's enough for now."

She smells like sweat and sunscreen instead of the lavender she always favored, and she feels different somehow, but then she would, wouldn't she, after four and a half years apart? I'm older and heavier and four inches taller than when we last hugged. Now I'm taller than she is. This must feel as strange to her as it does to me.

She finally chokes out, "Oh no, please no! It's true then."

A very un-Mom-like thing to say.

Her Zimbabwean English accent is much stronger than I remember. I release her and pull back enough to look at her face.

Amy Robinson's green eyes. Amy Robinson's freckles. Her hair, sun-bleached now to a lighter shade. But there's a scar on her upper lip that I don't remember, and a mole on her right cheek, and when she wipes the tears from her cheeks and her gaze meets mine, there's something I don't recognize in her eyes.

"Mom?" I shouldn't have to ask, should I?

"Oh Amelia, I'm so sorry."

Twenty

My arms drop to my sides, and I step back. "I don't know any Amelia."

What kind of new torture is this? She has probably had plastic surgery. Maybe *they* created this woman who looks like Mom to get information out of me. Information I don't have.

"I'm Tanzania Grey," I growl. "Who the hell are *you*?"

The woman shoots a quick glance at Pratt and Lyman and Bash, takes a shaky breath, wipes her hands on her shirt, and then tries to compose herself as her gaze returns to my face. "I'm Penelope Anne Patterson."

I so expected her to tell me that she was Amy Robinson that it takes a few seconds for this name to register.

Penelope? Isn't that a made-up name just for characters in books? Nobody is really named Penelope, are they? Penelope Anne Patterson?

"P.A. Patterson?" I grab hold of her sleeve. "*You're* P.A. Patterson?"

She nods. Her eyes—Mom's eyes—look into mine. "Didn't Piper, I mean your mum, tell you she had a twin sister?"

Piper? What the hell? "If you mean my mom, Amy Robinson, the answer is no." *Twin sister?*

My head is reeling. I can't tear my eyes away from her face. *Please, Mom. I want you so badly to be Mom.*

A tear slides down her cheek, and she wipes it away with the back of her hand. My face is wet, too, and she raises a hand toward me, but then leaves it hovering in mid-air. "Oh, Amelia..."

"Shhh," I hiss automatically, glancing over my shoulder at Bash and the squirrels. All six eyes are still on us, but I don't think they can hear what we're saying.

Mom was a twin? So no wonder, on the vid... A lightning bolt of disappointment flashes through me, leaving my ears ringing and my heart aching. I so wanted to find my mom alive.

Apparently Penelope was hoping for the same outcome, because her voice cracks as she murmurs, "My sister is really dead?"

It's my turn to nod. We are a pair of tragic bobblehead dolls.

She tilts her head slightly, presses her lips together for a second before asking, "And Alex?"

"Dad, too. Four years ago."

She squeegees tears from her cheek with the heel of her hand this time. "I so hoped..."

And then she breaks down into sobs again. And so do I, because she looks so much like Mom but she's not Mom, and that means my foolish hope that my parents might be still alive is just that: foolish. Futile. Epochally stupid.

She puts a gentle hand on my non-bandaged shoulder. My emotions ricochet around the interior of my skull.

I want her to hold me.

I don't want her to touch me.

My brain has been teleported to a different dimension. Suddenly, it's just too much, seeing Mom in front of me who is not really Mom. The woman in front of me is replaced by that horrible vision I saw four and a half years ago, the bodies of my mother and father swimming in pools of blood on our living room floor, and once again I watch two men dressed as ninjas, all in black except for that brief stripe of tattooed neck visible between mask and shirt on one, as they drag Aaron screaming from his room...

My legs threaten to collapse. Then Bash's arms wrap around me, keeping me from falling. The Secret Squirrels are a few steps behind him.

I wipe tears from my cheeks and take a deep breath. "This is Sebastian Callendro," I tell Not-Mom.

She looks him in the eye. "I know. The President's Son."

I feel Bash wince.

"I'm glad you're here with ... Tanzania," she tells him, switching my name after a brief hesitation. She holds out a hand.

Bash shakes it, then tells the guards that she's an old family friend and we deserve some privacy. Once again, the Secret Squirrels retreat.

She turns back to me. In a soft voice, she asks, "What happened, sweetheart?"

Bash's arms stiffen around me, and suddenly my guard goes up. Is this woman really my aunt, or is she trying to find out what I know about those ninja killers? There's so much she hasn't explained. Nothing makes sense.

"How did you know me?" I ask. With my caramel-colored skin and black hair, nobody would ever mistake me for my freckle-faced, chestnut-haired mother, and I haven't used my real name for over four years now.

Her gaze flits uncertainly to Bash and then back to my face.

"It's okay," I tell her. "Sebastian knows everything. Well, everything I know."

She swallows and then says, "Piper used to send photos of you and Aaron, and I knew she changed her name."

"You're telling me my mom was not really Amy Robinson?"

"Amy is Piper's middle name. Was." Penelope's eyebrows dip and her jaw trembles and she looks like she's about to burst into tears again, but finally she says, "As far as I know, your father's real name is—was—Alex Robinson."

Thank you, Almighty-Being-If-There-Is-One, for that. At least my birth name is real. "I know Mom used to be Amy Jansen."

It's P.A.'s turn to look confused. "Jansen? Is that what she told you?" She shakes her head. "No, we had friends named Jansen, but our family name is Patterson. Piper Amy and Penelope Anne. Two P.A. Pattersons."

I'm trying to decide whether to be angry about this additional lie when she says, "Your mum probably made up that Jansen detail to protect you."

"Protect me from what?"

"Wait." Bash steps between us. He aims a finger at Penelope. "None of that explains how you know that Tanzania Grey is Amelia Robinson."

This is starting to sound like a convoluted conversation in a really bad stage play, but he's right.

Penelope tucks a strand of her hair behind an ear. "Years ago, I saw an article about an extreme endurance race in South America. One of the photos looked exactly like the last picture Piper sent me of Amelia."

I remember that article: the Jungle Ultramarathon in the Amazon, my first multi-day endurance race. I was barely sixteen. I acquitted myself quite well, I'm proud to say, coming in second the first year and then winning the women's division the year after that. I still dream about anacondas slithering among giant water lilies.

"That's why I wrote to you," Penelope tells me. "I thought you'd recognize my name and the gifts I sent. Your mum and I had identical necklaces, so I sent you mine."

"A carved seed, strung on an elephant hair braid?"

She does the bobblehead thing again. "An outline of Africa, with a giraffe and a monkey and a bird carved inside."

She described it perfectly. I bobble back.

"Then, when you didn't respond to my messages, I thought maybe I was wrong about you. The invitation to this race was my last attempt to connect."

Guilt floods through me. I thought P.A. Patterson was an enemy all these years, maybe an ally of the ninja killers, trying to trap me into revealing my real identity. To think that I could have had a relative on my side, someone to talk to and to help me... But how could I have known? There are so many secrets in my screwed-up life, I don't know where to start. "Penelope, I—"

"Everyone calls me Penny," she interrupts. "You can call me Aunt Penny if you want." Another tear spills from her eye and streaks down her cheek. She wipes it away with her fingers. "Your grandmother is gone, I'm afraid, but you'll want to meet your grandfather, won't you? I know he'll want to meet you. He lives in Johannesburg."

My emotions crash into each other again. Elation: I have an aunt and a grandfather. Devastation: Mom and Dad are finally really truly gone. Forever. And there were never any Jansen relatives. A demolition derby is underway in my head.

A photographer emerges from the bushes nearby and snaps a photo of us standing here, Bash and I in our race clothes with our medals still hanging around our necks, Penny in her khaki uniform shirt, two of us with tears streaking down our faces, Pratt and Lyman lurking in the background.

"Shite!" Penny exclaims, which I guess is the way they pronounce it here. She yells something angry in another language at the photographer, and our Secret Service duo strides in the guy's direction.

"That was probably my fault," Bash tells her.

"Don't be so sure," she mysteriously responds. Then Penny jams her hat and sunglasses back on, grabs my arm and looks up at Bash. "Let me take you back to the dormitory. You've got to be exhausted."

Then she glances around warily. "Well, back to Victoria Falls, anyway. I'll have to let you out before we get to the race camp. It's not safe to be seen with me; Pattersons are still pretty much personas non grata around here."

The Secret Squirrels are returning to us after chasing away

the photographer. Before I can ask about the personas non grata comment, Bash murmurs, "Better idea. We go back in the plane like we're supposed to. That way nobody will be suspicious."

I whirl around, irritated by his attempts to protect me. "But I need to hear everything from...Aunt Penny." That last part still doesn't seem real to me.

"And you will," she promises. "But Sebastian is correct; we should stick to the original plan. Can you join me tomorrow, after you are released from the race camp?"

For this, for some final answers to the story of my life? Of course I can. New plane tickets and hotels will cost a fortune, but that's what credit cards are for, aren't they? Sabrina and Aaron and my boss at the zoo won't be happy, but somehow I'll make it work. "I'll stay."

Bash's forehead creases, and I'm reminded that he has a life of his own. Is he thinking of Mandy? Or maybe of college and his research project? If he leaves, his guards will go with him, and that will make it easier for me to travel without an entourage.

"No problem for you to go," I tell him. "You've got things to do."

"I'll stay," he states, his jaw hardening. Then he whispers, "I'll ditch the spooks."

Penny nods and whispers back, "When we're safe in Jo'burg, I'll tell you the whole story. Well, the part of the story I know, anyway. I'll meet you tomorrow morning near the entry gate to Victoria Falls Park."

"Eight a.m.?" Bash suggests.

"Make it nine so there will be a lot of tourists around for distraction," Penny says. "Blue Audi. Don't tell anyone you're meeting me. Good-bye for now." She turns away.

Suddenly I can't stand to let her out of my sight, and I clamp onto her forearm like an octopus snagging a fish. When she turns back, her eyes glitter with tears, and I know mine are watering again, too.

"I know," she whispers, and briefly puts both arms around me. "I *will* be there tomorrow morning, I promise."

"Me, too," I croak.

Before she turns again to vanish into the bushes, I notice that the embroidered patch on her shirt says *Médecins Sans Frontières*. Doctors Without Borders. I guess she'll explain that tomorrow.

Twenty-One

The next morning, the Secret Squirrels are waiting in the hall when I emerge from our dorm room. I'm wearing my PJs, a towel over my shoulder and my duffel bag in my hand as I head for the shower.

"He'll be right out," I tell them.

I almost feel sorry for them. It can't be pleasant to be assigned to keep tabs on someone who doesn't want to be guarded. Plus, I know that right at this minute, Bash is sliding out our dorm room window.

After I change clothes, I slip through the window in the women's room, and mix into the crowd of tourists gathered around the Victoria Falls Park gate. I spy my aunt in the parking lot in an old blue Audi. It still jolts my heart to see that familiar face, leaving me feeling like I've been punched in the chest. When I slide into the passenger seat to her left, I see Bash is already sprawled across the back seat, a ball cap over his face as if he's sleeping there. Sticking to the left lane, an insane practice this country apparently inherited from the Brits, Penny drives us to a rural airfield where a number of small planes are tethered. She tosses us and our luggage into a red and white Cessna, which has a normal configuration with the pilot's equipment on the left. Then she does a bunch of technical checking of gauges and toggles, and finally maneuvers us out into a field.

"You're a pilot?" Bash, obviously having lost his ability to reason, asks admiringly from the back seat.

"I sure hope so," I murmur, studying the dirt strip ahead of us that passes for a runway.

Penny chuckles. "In Africa, one needs to be. So many of the roads are simply shite, especially during rainy season. Your mother knew her way around a cockpit, too."

What? Mom knew how to fly?

Did Dad really know Piper Amy Patterson? Did any of us?

Penny takes a quick look around, then revs the engine to a low roar and we zoom down the dirt strip without announcing ourselves to anyone, which seems a bit alarming. Not to mention it's my first time in a tiny plane like this one. It feels as flimsy as a takeout box from a Chinese restaurant, and the sign on the strut says *Rent-a-Plane*. I shout over the noise, "Don't we need clearance or something?"

"Not to worry." Penny shouts back. "It's Africa."

Which somehow makes me worry even more.

The small plane leaps into the air like an ungainly heron. I wait for the usual clunk of wheels rolling up, but then I remember that the miniscule ones under us probably don't. We dip and slip sideways a couple of times, which makes me tighten my grip on the door handle.

"It's likely a good idea to let loose of the release, Amelia,"

Penny tells me in a loud voice. "No reason to open the door up here."

Open the door? I yank my hand over to my thigh, wipe off the sweat on my pants leg. It would be nice if this seat had armrests to hang onto, but there's nothing. I finally hook one hand in the safety belt in my lap, trying to appear nonchalant.

"First time in a small plane?" my aunt guesses.

"She white-knuckled it the whole time on the helicopter ride over Victoria Falls," Bash thrusts his head between our two seats to tell her. "I have the fingernail marks on my arm to prove it."

I want to punch him, but that would mean twisting around, which seems like it would jiggle the plane more. I yell, "The plane that took us back to Victoria Falls yesterday was a lot bigger." With half the competitors gone, there was even space for Lyman. I guess Pratt drove the Land Rover and drone back to the race camp.

"Yes, I've flown that model too." She turns her head to smile at me. "No worries; I'm an excellent pilot. I haven't seriously crashed in twenty-five years of flying."

Seriously crashed? Can you minorly crash? I'm afraid to ask.

"Eland." Now Penny's staring out her side window instead of watching in front of us.

I dare to look at the scenery below, and she's right, I see a herd of the huge antelope running across a clearing below, pursued by the shadow of our plane. They are joined by some smaller species; maybe gazelles of some sort.

When Africans fly across the United States, what do they

marvel at? Cities? Roads? I don't think there's anywhere in my country except maybe Alaska where you could see herds of any creatures moving across the landscape. That thought makes me sad, and I think about the elephant herd Bash and I encountered. They are hemmed in everywhere, and hunted by poachers, too. My heart aches for Bailey and his kin.

It will take us nearly five hours to make it to Johannesburg. About an hour in, it hits me that there is no place to pee on this small plane. I lean as close as I can to ask Penny about that.

She rummages under her seat and then holds up a plastic container with a screw-on lid.

"You're kidding."

"Practice makes perfect. I can piss in a thunderstorm."

Darn good thing that I didn't drink too much coffee or juice this morning. Bash takes the container from her and soon we hear gushing sounds from the back seat. Penny lifts an eyebrow in my direction and loudly comments, "As my mum used to say, a penis is a most convenient thing to have along on a picnic."

That statement could be taken a couple of different ways. My face flames up and I turn back to try and spot more animals down on the ground.

I'd hoped to find out more about my family from Penny, but the drone of the engine and whistle of air past the windows makes it too hard to carry on a conversation. Shouting our family secrets doesn't seem right. Soon, lulled by the white noise and undulations of the flight and still exhausted from the race, Bash and I are both asleep.

We wake up when we touch down at the small airport in South Africa. We check in, get our passports stamped, and then take a taxi to a neat brick house in a lush suburb. On the way there, I text Sabrina and my boss at the zoo that I won't be home for another few days. It's the middle of the night on the west coast of the U.S., and my housemate will still be asleep. I'm glad I don't have to look at Sabrina when I send that message, because I know she's been counting the minutes until I get back.

I always picture grandparents as stooped white-haired folks, but my grandfather, Ewan Patterson, is tall and muscular, and his dark hair and trim mustache have only a few threads of silver. I've never met anyone named Ewan before, which he pronounces as "You-an." I had to ask him how to spell it.

My grandfather's handshake is firm as he greets Bash. "Sebastian Callendro, the famous President's Son."

"Not so famous now that there's a new president," Bash says. "And for that, I'm grateful."

"I imagine the spotlight can be glaring," the older man says, sounding quite British. Then he turns to me. "So you are Amelia." His strong hands grasp my shoulders. "At last." He pulls me into an embrace, and I rest my face against his lean shoulder. My eyes are leaking again, wetting his crisp yellow shirt. I've never had a grandfather before.

When the pressure of his arms lessens, I straighten, and we back away from each other. His eyes are glittering, too, and he sniffs as he smoothes his thumb and forefingers down his mustache. Then he claps his hands. "Tea is in order, I think. Marianne?"

He looks toward the kitchen. A dark-skinned face peeks around the door frame. "Tea's coming, Mr. Patterson."

An expression of surprise flits across his face, but then he recovers and gestures toward the sofa. "Sit, sit."

Bash and I occupy the cushions as he hugs his daughter. "Penny dear, it's been too long. Where have you been?"

"Uganda," she says. "Rwanda. And Mozambique."

"You're with *Médecins Sans Frontières*? Doctors without Borders?" I ask. I so admire that organization because they send medical help into the most dangerous zones on the planet. "You're a doctor?"

"Yes to the first question. No to the last." Penny plops down into an armchair. My grandfather sits in the other as she explains, "I am sometimes a pilot and always a communications specialist. I write newspaper articles and informational pamphlets. I produce videos, I speak to the press. I coordinate deliveries of medical supplies and transportation and such. My sister and my father were the medical pros." She inclines her head toward her father.

"Pharmacist," he supplies.

I nod. "So that's where my mother got her interest in biochemistry."

His face stiffens for a few seconds and he looks toward the window, and I know he's thinking about Mom. Aunt Penny must have told him that Mom—his daughter Piper—is gone forever. It's nice to know someone shares my grief, but I feel guilty for bringing this heartache into this house.

He strokes his mustache again, recovering his composure,

and then his blue-eyed gaze connects with mine. "Will I meet Aaron?"

The question startles me for a second, and I pause to consider it. Aaron might be able to handle meeting our grandfather, but I don't think I can introduce him to Penny yet. A Mom Lookalike could easily shatter his fragile hold on reality. "Not right away."

"Oh?"

I've only just met my aunt and grandfather. How can I explain everything that's happened over the last four and a half years to me and my brother? "It's complicated."

"Indeed," he agrees.

"Tea, Mr. Patterson." Marianne enters, carrying a tray crowded with a teapot, cups, cream, sugar, silverware and a plate of cookies. The ensemble looks heavy. Bash stands up to take it from her.

"Oh for pity's sake, Marianne," my grandfather says. "Pull up a chair and stop acting like the maid."

The woman presses her lips together in embarrassment, but walks to the dining area and carries in a chair, placing it beside my grandfather. He holds out his hand and she takes it. Seeing black fingers intertwined with white fingers reminds me of Mom and Dad, and I try to sort out whether that sight brings me joy or pain. Both, I guess.

"In Zimbabwe," my grandfather explains, shifting his gaze from me to Bash and back, "Marianne was our housekeeper. But she was kind enough to come with me to South Africa after Laura...died."

"Mother was murdered," Penny interjects.

Grandfather swallows hard, blinks a couple of times, and then continues, "And now Marianne and I have become quite close. We plan to be married at Christmas."

Penny beams at both of them. "About time, Father."

"Congratulations," Bash and I say at the same time. I wonder what you call your grandfather's wife who isn't your grandmother. I'm not sure yet what to call *him*, either. Grandpa? Granddad? Grandfather? Ewan?

"Thank you." Marianne pulls her fingers from Mr. Patterson's and gestures toward the tea tray. "Please, help yourselves."

Bash pours tea for all of us, and we pass around the cookie plate—gingersnaps, my favorites—and then we settle back into our seats. Silence hangs thick in the air for a moment before my grandfather says, "When my daughters were small, we had a very nice house just outside of Victoria Falls. There was already political trouble when the girls were born, but mainly in Harare, and we were far from that. Then everything got worse over the next few decades."

"I've read about the hyperinflation and the food riots," Bash offers.

"Me, too," I say, although I only know that the history of Zimbabwe is sad. And bloody. Mom never shared any details.

My grandfather nods, probably grateful that he doesn't have to explain every horror that was committed by the government. "Piper studied in Johannesburg and in London, too. She was quite the prodigy, and she landed a job at the government lab in Victoria Falls doing biomedical research. We were so proud of her."

I glance at Penny, who is staring at her teacup as if reading a fortune in the leaves. I wonder if she's frustrated that her father is praising only her sister, or if she's just remembering my mom.

My grandfather takes a sip of tea. "Ebola was a problem over all of Africa in those days, and Piper and a colleague, Andrew Gambel, were working on developing medicines for it. They came up with an effective vaccine to prevent the early stage of the disease."

I tell them, "She worked on Ebola in the U.S., too."

Penny holds up a hand in a stop gesture. "Here, I mean in Zimbabwe, The Leader shut down the research."

Bash looks at her. "Why?"

"Medicine is power," Marianne explains. "And our government was interested only in power."

Grandfather continues, "The Leader wanted to control distribution of the vaccine; help his friends, let his enemies die. Piper and Gambel protested. They went to the press"—he looks at Penny at this point, so I gather she was somehow involved—"and everything blew up. Gambel was killed, the government seized our property, and The Leader's goons beat my beautiful Laura until she died." He takes a deep breath, lets it out in a sigh. "Penelope became the vagabond she is today, Marianne and I fled here, and Piper left the country."

Penny meets my eyes again. "Piper had met your father at an NGO conference, and you were already on your way."

This statement confuses me for a minute, but then I deduce that she means Mom was pregnant with me. I was conceived in Zimbabwe?

Grandfather takes Marianne's hand again. "And here we are," he summarizes.

For a long moment nobody says anything as they all stare at me. I realize it's my turn.

"In the U.S., Mom worked for a company called Quarrel Tayson, and she developed this vaccine for Ebola called Retaxafal 44."

"Ah," Penny says, "RT44."

"And this medicine called Plactate that goes along with the vaccine. So Mom did go on to actually prevent Ebola," I summarize. I am so proud of her.

"I *thought* Piper might have been involved in that." Grandfather's eyes light up with pride for a few seconds before his expression collapses back into sadness.

"But as you know"—I look toward Penny as I say this— "new strains of Ebola keep cropping up, and the company has to continually modify Mom's original vaccine to handle those. So she was uber busy keeping up with all of that."

"Of course she was," Marianne says. "Not to mention raising two children."

"Yes." A twinge of guilt tweaks my gut. I always remember Mom's work at the lab, but I don't give her credit for all the work she put into being a mom. "Dad worked as an accountant. He used to say that Mom was responsible for Quarrel Tayson's never-ending revenue stream."

Bash nods, agreeing. "Quarrel Tayson Corporation is one of the largest and most profitable companies in the world."

"How did she die?"

Although I should have anticipated the question, it still

startles me, and I turn to look at my grandfather. His eyes shine with tears, and the muscles of his face are rigid as he waits for my answer.

It takes me a moment to screw together enough courage to tell the rest. I've only told this story to two people, Sabrina and Bash. The President's Son reaches over now and takes my hand in his, squeezing it gently. That helps, but I still have to say it all in a rush just to get it over with.

"I was out late and I came home and looked through our back window before I opened the door. I saw Mom and Dad lying on the floor in pools of blood."

My grandfather stares into his teacup. "How long ago was this?"

"Four and a half years ago."

He and Marianne share a look as if that time period is meaningful.

Marianne sets her empty cup on the table between us. "Were they killed with knives?"

And it suddenly hits me, how little I know about my parents' deaths. I never even made it into the house. I shake my head and try to clear the sudden obstruction in my throat. "There were these ninjas—"

"Ninjas?" my grandfather interrupts, his eyebrows lifted.

Of course, how stupid, the killers are ninjas only in my mind. "Men dressed in black with masks over their faces—and they were dragging Aaron out of his room and he was screaming and then they saw me and chased me—"

It's suddenly all so vivid again, running for my life through the dark neighborhood, the fence blocking my way ahead, the headlights closing in on me, Aaron's screams echoing in my head. My esophagus ties itself into a knot and I lean into Bash's arms, trying to stifle my sobs against his shoulder.

Bash finishes for me. "So that's why Amelia became Tanzania Grey. A Hispanic family eventually took her in, but Amelia's basically been on her own for the last four years. She and Aaron got separated. We only located him eight months ago."

"Would Aaron know how Piper and Alex were murdered?" my grandfather presses.

I lift my head to stare at him in horror. I pray my brother didn't see my parents' murders. I will never ask him.

Through a blur of tears, I watch Penny lock eyes with her father, and then she says something in another language. It sounds like a cuss word. "The Leader's henchmen always used knives," she explains to us. "He was calling the shots right up until the day he died."

"Even here in Johannesburg, we would receive packages containing threatening notes and parts of dead animals, up until about four years ago," Marianne adds.

My grandfather says, "We thought The Leader simply got old and forgetful enough that he let it go. But now we know he was leaving us alone because he finally got his revenge in America." He shakes his head and sighs heavily.

Penny sniffs and brushes her fingers across her eyes. "Hell will never be hot enough for that monster."

Can that really be the explanation for my parents' murders? It seems farfetched to think the ninjas would travel all the way from Africa to kill an American family.

And if The Leader dropped out of sight almost a year ago, why have drones photographed my house and why have mysterious threats slithered into my life since then? What about the venom Maxine Newsome spewed about Mom's behavior at QTL? That creepy Phineas Pederson from Bellingham? Did he work for The Leader? The answer to all these questions can't be as simple as revenge from Zimbabwe's leader, can it?

I have so many questions, I can't think where to start. And I don't want to dump any more downers into the dark atmosphere. The sorrow in this room is already so thick you need a snowplow to drive through it.

"The hell with tea," Grandfather declares. He leaps up, vanishes into the kitchen, and returns with two bottles of wine and a corkscrew. Marianne retreats for a minute and returns with five glasses.

"Amelia, Tanzania, we will call you whichever you choose. And you will call me Grand."

Penny raises a sandy eyebrow at him, an expression that so reminds me of my mother, it almost makes me break into tears again.

"I like the sound of that. Grrrand." The trill he adds to the R makes the name sound Scottish.

"I do, too, Grand," I assure him. "And Tana is best for now, I think." When am I going to tell them all that I believe my parents' murderers may still be after me? When am I going to tell them about what happened to Aaron? It all seems so paranoid and insane right now, but if I can't tell my aunt and my grandfather, who can I tell?

As I dither about all this, Marianne pours the wine, filling each glass nearly to the top. My grandfather—Grand—picks his up. "To family. And friends."

I squeegee the tears from my cheeks, hold up my glass, and repeat, "To family and friends."

The red wine tastes rich. Its warmth sooths my sore throat. We have an early dinner of roast beef and potatoes and asparagus, topped off by a white cake with raspberry jam between the layers. Grand tells us entertaining wildlife stories. Marianne and Penny tell some funny stories of the Pattersons' life growing up in Zimbabwe that make me wish I could have known them all then.

Bash describes his mortification about discovering as a teenager that he was the result of an affair between the U.S. President and his Cuban mother. I tell them about Bailey, and they are incredulous that anyone would choose to keep a full-grown elephant as a pet. We laugh, we all get buzzed by the wine and the reunion.

Marianne shows us to the guest room, which has only one bed. But Bash and I are too tired and too smashed to protest, and I'm not even sure that we want to. That *I* want to, anyway.

We crawl into bed, Bash in his boxers and me in my PJs. He spoons me, nestling his chin on my shoulder. Physically, it feels good. Emotionally, I'm too wrung out to react.

"Congratulations," he murmurs in my ear.

I'm hovering just above unconsciousness, but I manage to whisper, "For what?"

"You have family in Africa."

That makes me smile, and at this moment, I feel richer

and luckier than I have felt for longer than I can remember. "Yes. I have family in Africa."

Everything else can wait until tomorrow.

Twenty-Two

The next morning, Penny's brushing her hair, studying her reflection in the mirror when I approach the guest bathroom. It still gives me a shock to see Mom-Not-Mom's face right in front of me. How long will it take me to get used to that?

"I adore those QTC products." Penny points a finger at the mint green bag of lotions I left on the countertop last night. Her nails are clipped short, in keeping with her no-nonsense personality. "And those bags are so clever as well. Seems like every Quarrel Tayson representative I run into has them."

I nod. "They spread them around quite a bit. Mine was a gift from QTC after a big race in Bellingham."

"I wish they'd spread one my way; the women from QTL are always passing them off between themselves. I like the orange bags the best, but those always seem destined for someone else."

I tell her she can have my green one. "I broke off the zipper pull, but it's still a pretty cool bag."

"That's nice, sweetheart, but I don't want to take yours."

Hearing my Mom Lookalike call me 'sweetheart' makes my throat constrict, and I have to swallow hard to keep my eyes from filling.

"I'll just pilfer one of those orange bags one of these days." She grins at herself in the mirror. Then she turns my way. "Oh sorry, Amelia, er, Tana, the lav's all yours." And she scoots toward the door.

After breakfast—eggs and bacon and coffee—Marianne and Grand bring out the family scrapbooks. It's bittersweet to see the photos of my mom and Penny and Grand and the grandmother I'll never get to meet. I trace a finger over a photo of a childhood foot race in which my mom is passing a baton to Penny. Or it might be the other way around; they are dressed in identical track suits, and both have their hair in ponytails.

"They were twelve years old there," Grand tells me.

"I had to slow down so Piper could catch me," Penny brags.

Although it's a remarkable example of stop-action photography for its time, the image disturbs me. It's too much like the creepy picture an intruder left behind at my home: a photo of me at age ten or so, passing off an egg in a spoon to my little brother Aaron during a QTL company picnic. Whoever left that photo in my yard wants me to understand that *they* know who Aaron and I are. It's kind of like finding a recently shed cobra skin on your front step; the clue isn't so frightening by itself, but it signals that danger is lurking close by.

This train of thought reminds me that I want Penny and Grand's help with the few clues my parents left behind, so I bring out my tablet, plug in the USB drive, and show my grandfather and Aunt Penny the work photos, the scans of spreadsheets and chemical lists. In the photos, they don't recognize anyone except Mom and Dad, and neither of them understand the alphabet soup list of chemical notations any better than I do.

"A friend says they are DNA sequences," Bash tells them. "Almost the same gene, with only slight differences."

Their expressions remain as blank as mine. However, Grand asks if he can send the spreadsheet to the printer in his study, so we do that and then he and Penny flatten the printed page on the table between them and study it for several minutes.

Grandfather taps the name at the top of the page. "What is World Cargo West?"

"That's an import-export company my dad did a lot of accounting work for," I tell him. "They transport packages around the world. Quarrel Tayson Labs, the company Mom worked for, used World Cargo West to ship stuff everywhere."

"I know they've delivered supplies for MSF," Penny says.

Bash interjects, "Or at least they used to."

He's reminding me of what I found out last year. "I'm not sure the company even exists anymore. I tried to find their office in Bellingham, but it's not there now. I think they went out of business after one of their major clients were caught importing cocaine from Colombia."

"This looks like standard expense accounting to me." Grand points to the column headings on the page. "Deliveries, costs." His forehead creases as he gazes up at me, frustrated at not finding more.

If it was *obvious*, I want to whine, I could have figured it out myself! But I keep my lips pressed together, saying nothing.

Penny's still studying the notations. "I believe RRT stands for Rapid Response Team. That's what Quarrel Tayson calls their researchers who zoom into each area after a new outbreak, yeah?"

"Yeah," I echo. I've heard the term often enough on the news. QTL's Rapid Response Teams are always hailed as heroes, and rightfully so, because who else would go willingly into an area where people are infected with Ebola?

She taps the sheet of paper. "And CD must stand for Courier Delivery. Each CD here happens just a few weeks after each RRT to the same location. That makes sense, because after the Rapid Response Team analyzes a new strain of Ebola, then QTL modifies the vaccine ASAP and flies it in to inoculate the local population. They are amazingly efficient."

"In other words, business as usual." Grand looks pained again. "Don't I remember your president awarding that Quarrel Tayson company a medal?"

"Yes." I stop there. I'm bitter about the way that was handled.

"Garrison awarded Quarrel Tayson Laboratories a Presidential Medal of Freedom," Bash tells Grand. "It's the only time a corporation has received it, for all the lives their Ebola vaccines have saved around the world."

"The CEO accepted the award," I tell my relatives. "He didn't even invite any of the scientists."

"Typical," Grand comments.

I don't want to dwell on that unhappy memory. I pull the printout of the spreadsheet around so I can look at it. Each CD notation is followed by two initials. I ask about those.

"Maybe the initials of the courier?" Penny guesses. "See, there are additional charges for flights, hotels, meals with those same initials."

"I met a courier in Bellingham last year," I tell them. "Elizabeth Abbott."

That's what the news called her when they reported her death, but when I met her, she called herself Liz. She was off to Casablanca, she told me, so excited to be a courier for QTL and deliver vaccines to exotic destinations. I wanted to join her. Then, less than two weeks later, her body was found by the side of the road in my hometown of Bellingham. I think that's why she haunts me. She was only a couple of years older, here and happy one day, her whole life erased only a short time later. I still have Liz's selfie on my cell phone, a confident young woman smiling into a mirror as she tried on her new QTC Cuties lipstick. As Penny mentioned earlier, QTL gave Liz one bag of cosmetics for herself and second to deliver to the QTL rep in Casablanca.

Penny taps the sheet on the table. "Did you ask Elizabeth about this spreadsheet?"

I shake my head. "She's dead. One day she was taking a side trip to Senegal to visit a friend, a few days later she got hit by a car in the States."

I'm sorry that I brought up Elizabeth Abbott. Now I'll never get her out of my head.

"Tragic." Grand sits back in his chair. "I'm sorry, but I just don't see anything out of the ordinary on that spreadsheet."

Penny slides back in her chair, too, so I guess she has reached the same conclusion.

If this piece of paper represents business as usual, why did my parents make an effort to scan and save it? This makes no sense.

"Some people at Quarrel Tayson Labs were really angry at Mom," I tell them. "There has to be a reason."

"Why do you think that?" Penny asks.

So I explain about how mom's co-worker Maxine Newsome said that Mom was going to ruin everything by talking trash about QTL.

Penny and Grand share a look. Then Grand turns to me. "I'd guess that was about money."

Aunt Penny nods. "When your mum found a vaccine for Ebola, she thought that everyone should get it, no matter who they were, no matter if they could pay or not. That's what got her into trouble in Zimbabwe."

Grand groans. "Had it been used right away, the vaccine that Piper created could have wiped out the disease in Zimbabwe. Maybe in all of Africa. Who knows what might have happened if her vaccine had been deployed immediately across the continent? It might have eradicated the disease before all these mutations started cropping up."

"But at least now there *is* a vaccine everywhere," I say. "RT44 goes around the world, over and over again, with hundreds of adaptations to immunize against new strains of Ebola. That all started with my Mom."

Grand wipes at his eyes. "That's my girl."

Marianne pats his arm in sympathy, then turns back to me. "As I said last evening, The Leader wanted to give the vaccine only to his supporters, and withhold it from his enemies. Piper thought that was immoral."

Grand groans. "She said so, on nationwide television." He shoots a dark look at Penny, who ducks her head.

"I helped a bit with that," she admits in a low voice.

"They broke into the national broadcast network! Piper looked right into the camera and said, 'Our leader refuses to share the cure for Ebola. The government of Zimbabwe is immoral.'" Grand shakes his head. "My poor naïve girl."

I point at him. "That's like one of the last things I heard her say. She was talking on the phone to someone at QTL, and she said, 'That's not only unethical, that's immoral.'"

"That sounds like Piper." Grand folds his arms across his chest. "And right she was, too, but one does not tell an all-powerful dictator that he is immoral. What good is morality if it gets you killed? It took nearly fifteen years, but The Leader hunted down my girl and finally got his revenge."

Is he right? Could my parents have been killed because of my mom's history in Zimbabwe? That seems unlikely. Because the problems didn't stop after Mom moved from Zimbabwe.

That's not only unethical, that's immoral. Mom was talking to someone at QTL. What could be so unethical and immoral there? I never heard of QTL withholding vaccines because of a lack of resources to pay for them. There are hundreds of articles about how QTL often foregoes profits to sell the vaccines to poor countries. The company has saved so many lives because they're able to adapt to each new outbreak so fast.

Could the power of an African dictator really stretch all the way to Bellingham, Washington, just to exact revenge for a political embarrassment that happened fifteen years earlier? Penny and Grand and even Marianne seem satisfied with this explanation. Am I just a naïve American?

I describe what happened to Aaron—the kidnapping, the drugs, the imprisonment, the resulting mental illness.

"That is absolutely horrific," Grand says sadly. "I'm so sorry all that happened."

"But why?" I ask.

"Maybe the murderers just couldn't kill a little boy," Penny guesses. "The Leader's thugs often spared children, if you want to call murdering their parents and abandoning them as orphans sparing them."

Then it hits her that she's just described exactly what happened to me and Aaron. Her hand flies to her throat and she hastily says, "Oh, Amelia."

"I've had years to adjust." Although I'm not yet accustomed to hearing my Mom Lookalike call me by my birth name. During this conversation, my neck muscles have grown so rigid, it feels like my head might snap off.

"Obviously, they found a way to prevent your brother from telling the truth." Penny remarks.

I don't believe that Aaron knows the truth. I certainly don't. I tell them about the drones that have invaded our privacy, and the time a helicopter landed and Bailey was nearly killed and my hairbrush vanished from the house.

Grand shakes his head. "My God. I don't know how you have coped with all that."

"Nothing has happened for a little more than six months now," I tell them. "I keep waiting for the other shoe to drop."

Grand and Marianne glance at each other, and then Marianne tells me, "That's when he died."

That remark makes no sense to me. "What?"

"When who died?" Bash asks. I'd nearly forgotten he was in the room.

"The Leader," Marianne says. "They forced him out of office over a year ago, but he didn't die until six months ago."

Can that really be the solution to all my problems? Is it possible that with the death of a brutal dictator in Zimbabwe that my brother and I will be safe from now on? It seems too easy, but I'd like to accept that explanation. It would be such a relief to live life without looking over my shoulder all the time.

Bash and I need to leave tomorrow, so my newfound relatives take us on a tour of local gardens and wineries and beautiful bluffs overlooking the sea. They whisk us by slums that we smell before we see, masses of dark-skinned humanity squeezed into tiny cement shacks. I'm reminded of that village we stayed in during the race, and of the shacks I lived in with Marisela's family while we picked crops in the fields. Poverty looks much the same, no matter which country it's in.

After dinner in the evening, I take my phone to our guest room to videochat with Aaron and Sabrina and tell them I will be on a plane tomorrow.

Penny wants to say hello to Aaron, but I have to tell her it's too soon. Seeing Mom-Who-Is-Not-Mom could easily splinter my brother's precarious sanity into a thousand sharp-edged shards. I don't have Aaron's problems, and still déjà vu smacks me every time I glance at Penny, leaving me feeling unbalanced and slightly dizzy, like the force of gravity has been altered.

"I can't wait for you to get back," Sabrina tells me. "Bailey's acting up."

"Yeah?" I'm not sure I want to hear this. It's akin to being told that Godzilla is having a bad day.

"He knocked down the garden fence and he circles the house each evening, looking in all the windows. He even wiped snot all over the front and back doors."

This is not good news. My elephant is clearly searching for me. What's next? He could push down the front door, or even a whole wall.

"Keep him distracted until I get back."

"With?" Sabrina demands, one pierced eyebrow lifted.

Aaron crowds in beside Sabrina, and I catch a glimpse of the early morning sunlight through the window behind him. The ten-hour difference is disorienting.

"Why are you late?" my brother asks.

"Because I have good news, sort of." I tell them that I've located some of our extended family, but I don't tell either of them that I'm staying with my grandfather and aunt. Aaron would have a million questions for Grand, and Grand would spill the beans for sure about his twin daughters. I have to come up with a plan to handle all of this.

"Bring them home with you," Aaron insists.

"It's not that simple, bro. Plus, we barely know each other.

And where would they sleep?"

"Marisela and Kai and Kiki are going home tomorrow," Aaron tells me. "Bring them."

Beside him, Sabrina is gritting her teeth. My brother is a handful, and it's not fair to expect her to be responsible for him.

I force a note of cheer into my voice. "Hang in there. Pet Bailey for me. I'll be back before you know it."

"You'd better be." Sabrina makes a sound somewhere between a growl and a sigh before she ends the call.

I'm not quite sure what to do with these bits and pieces of history I've gathered. Chalking up Mom and Dad's murders to revenge from The Leader doesn't feel like a satisfactory answer. It doesn't explain Maxine Newsome's bitterness and Phineas Pederson's ominous presence in my life. It doesn't explain the drones that haunt my home, the invasion by helicopter, or the photo of Aaron and me as youngsters. Unless somehow QTL was tied into The Leader's circle of nastiness? No, not even then. Mom was the star of the company. She made them zillions of dollars. They'd never get rid of her just for cold revenge. Unless, perhaps, they had no more use for her.

And what about Dad? Just collateral damage?

These thoughts swirl through my head as I brush my teeth for the night. After rubbing lotion into my face, I stuff the bottle back into my green QTC bag, thinking about how Penny wants an orange one. Maybe I could buy one for her. I try to picture the colors of bags I've seen in the QTC stores at the airports. Have I ever seen orange?

And then a memory projects onto the screen of my mind: Liz Abbott and me as we waited for the elevator in the QTL building. She held two QTC bags, and told me she liked the orange one best but had been instructed to give it to the QTL rep in Casablanca. After a sly wink, Liz divulged a secret: she had booked a secret side trip to Senegal on the way, to meet a friend there. "What they don't know, right?"

Click—next photo. Liz's selfie, showing her trying on lipstick in Senegal. Lipstick that most likely came from the *orange* cosmetics bag at her side.

Penny saying that the QTL couriers always had orange bags destined for someone else.

What's so special about the *orange* bags? Apparently, the QTL couriers carry them around the globe with instructions to hand them off to the reps at their exotic destinations. Liz apparently kept the orange bag because she liked it best.

And then Liz died two weeks later in a supposedly unrelated hit-and-run accident in Bellingham.

I assumed the contents of those orange cosmetics bags were the same as all the other QTC bags—lipstick, lotions, lip gloss, sunscreen. Obviously the lipstick was just a lipstick; Liz was applying it in the selfie. But what if the other containers were filled with something she wasn't supposed to discover?

Gold dust?

Illegal drugs?

Diamonds?

Was Liz's death an accident? Or was it because she stumbled on some secret smuggling operation that QTL was involved in?

My dad charted imports and exports around the world, movements of goods from Quarrel Tayson via World Cargo West. World Cargo West was later caught up in a scandal about importing heroin. Did Dad stumble onto the same secret that Liz had?

And my mom. *That's not only unethical, that's immoral.* What sort of immoral business was Quarrel Tayson involved in?

Did my parents die for the same reason that Liz did? If that's true, whatever vile deeds the giant corporation is practicing has been going on for at least five years. Quarrel Tayson Corporation owns every sort of business. It would be easy for them to distribute drugs or diamonds or gold to friends around the world.

I don't want to believe the strands of evil my imagination is braiding together.

Twenty-Three

"You okay, Tarzan?"

I'm catatonic, toothbrush halfway to my mouth. Looking into the mirror, I see Bash standing behind me. I didn't even hear him come in.

"Okay?" He touches my upraised arm.

"No." I spit into the sink, and rinse off my toothbrush. "Decidedly not okay."

"What the—" he starts.

I can't have this conversation in a bathroom. I drag him through the quiet house. Lights are off everywhere except for our room. Everyone else has gone to bed. I pull Bash out into the darkness of the patio and close the sliding doors behind us.

"Tana?" He frowns and crosses his arms. He's wearing a T-shirt and boxers, and both of our feet are bare against the flagstones. The evening air is getting cold. "You're worrying me."

"You know how I told you about Liz Abbott and that orange cosmetics bag?"

His face says *No.* Okay, even if I did tell him, it probably didn't register. "Liz Abbott, the courier who died?" I prompt.

"Yeah," he says. "She was carrying an orange bag of cosmetics that she was supposed to give to the QTL rep meeting her in Casablanca."

So I did tell him. But his expression is still blank.

"I think she switched that orange bag with the gift bag she was given."

He looks even more perplexed. "And?"

The door opens behind us, and I jump, startled. It's Penny, wearing a lilac colored robe and slippers. In the dim light, with her hair pulled back into a braid, she looks a little less like Mom. I'm grateful for that. Would it be uber selfish to ask her to dye her hair or cut it super short or something?

"What's going on?" my aunt asks.

Okay, I'll have an audience of two to hear my insane theory. "I think QTL is involved in something illegal. I think there's something important in those orange bags."

Understandably, she frowns and her lips flatten into a skeptical line. Bash mirrors her expression. So I tell them about how there was an orange bag in Liz Abbott's selfie in Senegal although she had been instructed to give that bag to someone in Casablanca.

"And then a couple of weeks later, Liz was killed in Bellingham." It chills my blood to say *kill* and *Bellingham* together again. Bellingham is my birthplace, but it's also my parents' death place.

Bash uncrosses his arms and rubs his chin thoughtfully. "A major corporation, smuggling? I don't want to believe it."

"I don't either," I reply. "Please tell me I'm insane."

"It *is* Africa," Penny says. "Where leaders are routinely bribed. Diamonds might make sense. A designer drug might make even more sense. QTL *is* a pharmaceutical company."

"Bribed for what?" Bash asks.

Penny flicks a hand in the air. "So many possibilities. Free passage, illegal wildlife trophies, major contracts ... It's actually brilliant. What better way to get bribes into a country than to import them with lifesaving vaccines?"

The three of us spend a moment just staring at each other. My brain is getting tired of trying to sort through all the possibilities.

"We have the perfect opportunity to test your theory," Penny remarks. "MSF cordoned off an outbreak area in northern Zimbabwe about ten days ago; that's why the race was shortened. I flew in QTL's analysis team six days before I flew to the finish line to meet you."

"How long does it typically take QTL to formulate a new vaccine?" Bash looks at me for the answer.

Like I would know.

Fortunately, Penny does. "A supply of vaccines usually arrives a week to ten days after the RRT takes samples of the new outbreak. I can find out when the courier is expected. We'll intercept that orange bag." She glances from Bash to me and back to Bash again. "I'll need your help."

We stand silently in the cool night air, letting the challenge soak in. Finally, after more than four years, I feel a spark of hope that maybe I've stumbled onto the reason my parents were murdered. Finding my voice again, I say, "Count me in."

Then it hits me that, shit, this means I will have to postpone my trip back to the States even longer. I am not looking forward to explaining that to Sabrina. Or to my boss at the zoo. Like the coward I am, I decide to put off those phone calls until tomorrow.

Bash's expression is grim, and I know he's thinking that although he arranged to be my race partner, he did not sign up for this. Whatever *this* might turn into.

Penny's face is pale and tight in the moonlight. She holds a finger to her lips. "Mum's the word. And now, to bed."

Like I could sleep. Back in our room, when Bash throws an arm around me in bed, his muscles feel as tightly wound as mine, like a coiled spring ready to explode.

"What?" I finally say.

He murmurs, "I hope you're wrong, Tana."

"Thanks for your support."

"How many people do you think work for the Quarrel Tayson companies?" he asks.

"Thousands, I'm sure."

"Make that hundreds of thousands. More like millions, if you count all the subsidiaries around the world."

Is he hinting that I should just let this go? That Quarrel Tayson should be allowed to carry on illegal activities because they employ a multitude of people? "That doesn't make it right, Bash."

"Of course not," he agrees. "But it makes it dangerous. The implications are ... financial. Political. International. Astronomical."

He's right, but his tone grates on me. Is he afraid he'll lose his sponsorship? The money for his precious mining research?

I believe that maybe I'm finally on the right path.

I can't stop now. I *won't* stop now. "I can't go home tomorrow."

After a long tense moment, he says, "Then I can't, either."

"Yes, you can. It's not your fight, Bash."

He rolls over, turning his back to me.

Twenty-Four

Two days later, we are at a tiny airstrip close to the Ebola quarantine area. There's only one runway, just a long section of ground that has been mowed and cleared of grass. A ramshackle hut serves as a terminal for anyone who has to wait here. Penny is wearing her MSF uniform and badge, and she's outfitted Bash and me as airport security staff, with nametags on navy epauletted uniform shirts that are long enough to conceal guns at our waists, which we don't have, or a plastic pouch of cosmetics, which, along with an empty plastic bag, is currently tucked into the front of my pants, making me look pregnant.

The more I discover about my aunt Penelope Ann Patterson, the more she reminds me of my adopted mom, Marisela Santos. Determined. Slippery. Seemingly, Penny can make almost anything happen. I wondered how she moved in and out of countries so easily if the Patterson name was so dangerous in Zimbabwe.

"The name on my passport is not Patterson," she informs

me. "I'm married to a man named Anton Joubert, who lives in Pretoria."

We've been together for days now, and not once has she mentioned a husband. "Really?"

"In name only," she confides. "Anton is homosexual, which is akin to a death sentence in many places in Africa. So he and I have a mutual protection agreement."

My aunt has even somehow arranged for a security scanner machine, although this one we brought with us yesterday is suspiciously small. There's no way a really big suitcase could pass through it. But then, maybe no big suitcases ever come in to this rural airstrip. 'Rustic' is the most complimentary term I can come up with for this location. A dim light fixture hangs from bare wires overhead, a rough bench and three rickety chairs line the walls. There are no conveyor belts, no moveable stairs to use with planes, not even a drinking fountain. A rickety outhouse serves as a restroom. I guess we're lucky the building has electricity supplied by a solar panel on the roof.

"Would an airport this small even have security?" *Airport* is a grandiose term for the place. And this seems like a hokey plan.

Penny shrugged. "It's Zimbabwe. You never know when you might get shaken down by some government goons. If The Leader wants it, it happens."

Bash blinked. "I thought The Leader was gone."

The look she gave him said he was naïve. "His legacy—and his henchmen—live on. Generations of Zimbabweans don't know any other system."

Yesterday, after setting up the scanner, we turned it on and ran a few items through it, practicing our drill. Then Penny locked up the terminal shack and took us to a local bar to soothe our jittery nerves. Turns out that in Zimbabwe the drinking age is eighteen, so I'm legal, even though nobody here seems to care. In South Africa, you can get a beer if you're sixteen. By comparison, the U.S. is downright Puritanical.

After dinner last night, Penny dumped Bash and me in a small RV campground—she called it a caravan camp—that rents out vehicles. Then she returned to the quarters she shares with other MSF personnel, promising to come back at ten in the morning to take us back to the airstrip.

We've been two days without a connection to 'net or email, which is either really bad or really good. When I told Emilio I was spending more time in Africa, he immediately asked, "With Callendro?"

Sabrina was prickly when I informed her I would not be home for a few more days.

But I can't think about what might be going on back in Washington State right now. Today's the day for the big switch, and if we don't get this right, we may never know if my theory is correct.

We couldn't find an orange cosmetics bag in the QTC shop at the Johannesburg airport, so we'll have to substitute the cosmetics the Quarrel Tayson courier brings for the ones in the plastic bag that is currently making my abdomen sweat. This could be tricky, but I remind myself that over the last four and a half years, I have become an expert at deception.

A Jeep roars up outside. Bash and I switch into acting

mode as Penny walks in with a woman she calls Elaine, who is the Quarrel Tayson employee assigned to take possession of the vaccines that are on their way.

Elaine looks more like a corporate type than a medical professional. Her pants and blouse have been recently pressed, and her hair is twisted up into a tight knot. After she glimpses Bash and me and our hokey scanner, she stops in her tracks. "What's this?"

Instead of sweating bullets, I'm covered in goose bumps. I'd rather face down another wild elephant than be here right now. I grit my teeth and remind myself that I'm doing this for Mom and Dad.

While I'm debating my next move, Bash authoritatively states, "By order of the government, madam, all incoming goods must be inspected." His slightly British African accent is surprisingly good.

Penny sighs dramatically. "They were here yesterday when supplies came in, too. Everything's got to go through the machine."

"Surely not medical supplies," Elaine insists, still glaring at us.

Bash glares right back. "Especially medical supplies, madam."

I narrow my eyes and frown to match his attitude. When I cross my arms in an attempt to appear more determined, the plastic bag in the front of my pants slips down an inch and makes a tiny crinkling sound. I sidestep to hide my belly lump behind the scanner.

"Damn government shakedown; I've heard they're

harassing all the NGOs." Penny shakes her head and makes a disgusted sound in the back of her throat.

I'm dithering about whether or not it would be wise to say anything when we hear a plane approaching, zooming our way less than fifty yards above the landing strip. I've learned this is routine, to make a low pass first over unattended rural landing fields, because there are often animals sunning themselves on the cleared areas, or local villagers playing soccer or drying clothes in the sun.

We all move to the doorway to watch the small plane buzz the field, and sure enough, a couple of rabbit-type creatures dart off into the tall grass at the side of the field, and a dark scaly ribbon zips across the open area so quickly I'm not sure whether I saw or just imagined a snake there.

The plane circles around and settles onto the runway without even a bounce, then slows and comes to a stop alongside our building.

The pilot, a handsome young man who doesn't appear any older than I am, gets out, along with a young woman in stretchy black yoga pants, sandals, and a long-sleeved blue tunic top. I can tell she's American before she even speaks, and I bet she's from Western Washington University, just like Liz Abbott was. Quarrel Tayson recruits college students as couriers. Like Liz did, she's carrying a metal briefcase. The pilot pulls out a backpack and follows her toward the terminal. I am about to ask her if she's from Bellingham when Bash gives me a vicious jab with an elbow, and we both move to the scanner to fulfill our acting roles in this scenario.

The courier steps into the building, shakes hands with

Elaine, and then hands the briefcase to her with a little bow. Their delivery ceremony seems overly formal, but, whatever—I guess it's the conclusion of official courier duty for this gal. Now she gets to go back to Harare or wherever this small plane came from, and spend the evening in an exotic locale. Liz Abbott was very proud of that benefit.

"I brought sodas." Penny extracts bottles of orange liquid from the little cooler she carried in. "They're still cold. Elaine?"

The Quarrel Tayson rep shakes her head.

Penny uncaps three and hands one to the courier and one to the pilot, who gratefully lifts it to his lips, saying "Ta," which sounds as if it might be short for "Thanks."

The courier starts to do the same, then yelps, "Oh, I almost forgot!"

She takes the backpack from the pilot, sets it on the ground, and extracts an orange bag from a front pocket. "This is for you, with compliments from the head office."

"Thank you, dear. You can be on your way now." Dismissing the courier and the pilot, Elaine tucks the bag under one arm and heads for the door on the opposite side of the room. Penny follows, her soda in hand, her expression strained.

Bash steps into Elaine's path, blocking her from the door. Gesturing toward the scanner, he says, "Madam, I must insist."

She tries a dismissive glower.

"I have my orders." He places a hand on the bulge at his hip and he's so convincing that even I worry he's reaching for a gun, until I remember he has his cell phone in a holder clipped to his belt there.

Elaine hastily sets down the briefcase. From her pants pocket, she pulls out a wad of cash, and hands it to Bash.

He shoves the bundle of bills into his front pants pocket. Elaine reaches for the briefcase, but Bash grabs the handle before she can. She puts a hand on each side of the case, and for a few seconds, they glare at each other like dogs that want the same toy.

Elaine is the first to blink. She reluctantly relinquishes the briefcase. Through clenched teeth, she snarls, "Be careful with that. Those are vaccines to save lives."

Then Bash holds out his hand for the cosmetics bag under her arm. She frowns. He gestures toward the scanner, and she moves in that direction.

I switch the machine on, and the short conveyor belt hums around its pulleys. Bash studies the briefcase, which has a built-in combination lock near the handle. "Open this, madam."

Is he overdoing the 'madam' bit? Who am I to criticize? I'm not doing anything at all. After Elaine aligns the locks and springs it open, exhaling dramatically to show her exasperation, I move to Bash's side and examine the contents. Hundreds of little ampoules, tucked into Styrofoam pockets. I pluck one out, hold it up to the light.

This time, it's Penny who hisses. "Be careful! That's glass."

I give her the most disdainful look I can muster, tuck the ampoule back into the case, and then place the case on the conveyor belt. It is sucked into the machine, and then automatically stops beneath the scanner. There's only a flimsy black curtain between my belly and the briefcase. Stepping into place behind the viewing screen, I see hundreds of little objects surrounded by a big metal container. I hope that's what a container full of vaccines is supposed to look like. Nodding as if I approve, I press a button and let the briefcase pass through to the other side.

"The bag," I say to Bash, inclining my head toward Elaine. To my anxious ears, those words did not sound in the least African, or even British, but they were only two words.

Elaine reluctantly gives up the orange cosmetics bag. Visibly tense, she watches as Bash places it on the conveyor belt and it is carried into the scanner. Her eyes are glued to the process and she starts to step around toward me so she can view the screen, too.

Crap! I'm not a magician; I can't do this with her watching me.

Then Bash shoves Penny into Elaine, splashing the orange drink Penny is carrying all over Elaine's blouse and pants. Penny drops the bottle on top of Elaine's foot for good measure. Soda radiates out in an orange splatter all over the cement floor.

"Shite!" Penny yanks the kerchief from her neck to mop off Elaine's neck and arm.

"Sorry, madam," Bash apologizes while pulling Penny by the arm to place her between the scanner and Elaine.

"Here, Elaine." Penny bends over to tug at Elaine's foot. "Ugh, let me have your shoe; I can rinse it off with some water. I *so* hope these are not ruined."

Elaine's gaze shifts toward the floor. I switch from audience to actor, pulling the cosmetics bag out, emptying its contents into my empty plastic bag, emptying the cosmetics I had stuffed into my pants into the orange bag. I've only just zipped it again when Elaine straightens and focuses on me. The substitutes are in the orange bag and the stolen cosmetics are in the bag in my pants, but I didn't manage to push the empty plastic bag into my waistband. Now it flutters to the floor beside my foot.

Shite, shite, shite! As Penny would say.

"What *are* you doing?" Elaine glares at me. "How long can it take?"

I narrow my eyes at her while I move my foot onto the plastic bag. My shoe slips a little. I hope my big foot is covering the evidence.

Whipping a cell phone out of her pants pocket, Elaine snaps a photo of us at the scanner. "The authorities are going to hear about this," she threatens.

Twenty-Five

Double shite. What does Elaine intend to do with that picture?

Penny attempts to help. "Don't waste your time, Elaine. I complained yesterday. To totally deaf ears."

"Are you *done*?" Elaine demands, her furious gaze raking over my tacky uniform and nametag.

Morris, I remind myself, I am *Morris*.

"Nearly finished, madam." I press the button to move the bag out of the machine, recover it with my left hand and pass it with my right to Bash, an awkward movement to be sure, but I don't want to move my foot or step away from the machine. One corner of sharp plastic is jabbing my abdomen. I suspect the bag I hurriedly stuffed into my pants now makes me look like I've got a sharp-hooved goat in my belly instead of a human fetus.

Bash hands the orange cosmetics bag back to Elaine, saying haughtily, "You may pass." His gaze motions her to the door.

She recovers her briefcase and tucks the orange bag under her arm, and says nothing as she exits the building. Outside, we hear her complain, "What a load of crap that was!"

Penny attempts an apology. "Dreadfully sorry about the soda, Elaine. I believe that clumsy clark tripped me on purpose. Really, this is *so* Zimbabwe. We always hope it will-"

They drive off, still discussing our insulting behavior and general ineptitude. On the other side of the building, we hear the plane rumble past and lift off.

Bash and I have the building to ourselves. I hurriedly yank the package of cosmetics from my pants and set it carefully on the conveyor belt, rubbing my abdomen. Then we both collapse onto a bench and simply breathe and stare at that bag for a moment. It's not one of the stylish QTC cosmetic travel bags, with translucent sides and colored edges and a fancy zipper, but a plain gallon-size ziplock baggie. All the bottles and tubes inside look innocent enough, but we've seen enough crime shows on television to know that we shouldn't touch them more often than we have to, because we might mess up fingerprints or DNA on them. Finally, Bash walks over to inspect the cooler Penny left by the door.

"One left." He pulls out a bottle of orange soda, rummages for the opener and uncaps it, then flops down next to me, offering me the first swallow. I take a big gulp and hand it back.

"We did it, Bash." I wish I had my own bottle to clink with his in celebration.

"Step One, done, madam," he agrees, using his fake African-English accent again. "Only ninety-nine to go."

"Enough with the madam bit." I wish he hadn't reminded me that we've only just begun what could turn out to be a deadly enterprise. If Bailey were here, he'd wrap his trunk around my shoulders. I could use a little elephant comfort right now.

My chest is tight with anxiety. "What if she sends that photo to someone?"

"Like who?"

"I don't know. Someone in authority. Someone nearby." I glance nervously at the doors, and then get up and check. Only the grass and trees are moving in the breeze outside. "Penny might not be back for hours."

"Then let's enjoy the peace and quiet while we have it," he says.

We take the two least rickety-looking chairs outside to enjoy the rest of our soda. Clouds are stacking up overhead, and I'm glad we're not flying today.

At first there's not much to watch, and I wish I'd brought a book or a magazine. I keep wondering about what Bailey and Aaron and Sabrina are up to at home right now. This is the longest I've ever been gone from my elephant and my brother. I have an unwelcome vision of Bailey and Aaron creating a pyramid of rocks and then climbing on them. Shocked neighbors spy an elephant on the horizon, and all hell—

A troop of baboons emerges from the tall grass, and I'm grateful for the distraction. The monkey family sits on the landing strip and grooms each other. Bash and I laugh at the antics of three youngsters. They find a lizard and toy with it, alternately attacking it and running away when it opens its mouth and hisses at them. Baboon kids are not so different from the human kind.

The sun is setting when we hear a vehicle approaching the other side of the shack.

"Finally!" Bash jumps up and carries his chair inside.

I follow. I am so ready to catch a ride with Penny and head for dinner and bed. It's been a stressful day.

Bash glances through the doorway at the approaching vehicle. Instead of walking out to greet Penny, he jumps backward. "Shit!"

He doesn't have to add that it's not my aunt. I grab the bag of cosmetics from the machine and we both run for the door on the opposite side of the building.

"Soldiers," he hisses under his breath.

Twenty-Six

Outside the building, we squat with our backs against the wall. We can't stay here. It's only a few short steps through the little building from the driveway side to our landing strip side. The vehicle engine shuts off and we hear two men enter the structure, talking to each other in a native language. Hugging the wall, we dash around the corner of the building to the back side.

Tall grass borders the hut on that side, an open field that stretches for at least a hundred yards before it reaches some scrubby trees. Tall grass that could be hiding snakes, or even lions. But we have no choice.

I quickly tuck my uniform shirt into my pants and shove the bag of stolen cosmetics down the neck onto my back, then we both dive into the tall grass and crawl on our bellies like crocodiles. We're only fifty feet in when we hear the voices of the soldiers behind us. Knowing that the grass would be waving over our heads at our movements, we stop and lie motionless, plastered against the ground.

A vivid flashback fills my brain. I close my eyes and I reach my hand out to grasp Bash's shirt. When The President's Son and I first teamed up on Verde Island, we were attacked in tall grass just like this. What followed was absolutely horrific. A giant spider was the least of it. It's a miracle we both survived. As we listen to the soldiers' banter back and forth, Bash gently removes my hand from his shirt and laces his fingers through mine.

At least the voices don't seem to be coming closer. The soldiers—it sounds like two—chat for a minute, joking around. When the gunshot comes, Bash and I both startle. Then there's more laughter, and the voices muffle. Maybe they're headed back inside?

What if they decide to drive around and inspect the airfield? When I look at Bash's face, I can see that he is thinking the same thing, so at a nod from him, we both take off again, crawling as fast as we can through the tall grass. The cosmetics bag slides around in the sweat on my back. It feels like I'm carrying a tortoise. With claws. We've barely reached the first trees when we hear the Jeep engine behind us. From the cover of some scrawny bushes, we chance a look at the landing strip.

Yep, these guys decided to drive over the airfield. They zip away from our position. But it seems likely they'll come back. I look up into the tree over our head, debating whether it would be safer to climb or to stay on the ground. If we climb, we might be more hidden, but if they spot us, we'll be easy targets.

The cosmetics have slithered halfway under my right arm, transforming my tortoise hunchback into an obscene growth emanating from my armpit. My back is covered with scratches from the sharp plastic corners. The skin there itches like crazy. I want to elbow the package back to the center of my back, but I'm afraid to move.

Through the cover of grass and shrubbery, we watch the Jeep race down the airstrip, stopping near the far end. One of the soldiers hops out and picks up a limp form. Dangling legs and dark fur.

"Baboon," I whisper. Based on its size, it's one of the youngsters. That must have been the gunshot we heard.

The soldiers share a laugh. Then one heaves the corpse into the back of the Jeep. Poor baby.

"What the heck happened to Aunt Penny?" I whisper, although of course I know Bash doesn't have any more answers than I do.

Penny had promised she'd be back in a couple of hours, and now it's been more than four. I try to tamp down the most horrible possibilities, but naturally my imagination goes there and I envision my Mom Lookalike swimming in a pool of blood just like Mom was the last time I saw her. My throat starts to close up, and I try to clear it, while attempting to dispel that awful image.

PTSD. The gift that keeps on giving.

After the soldiers loiter a few more minutes near the end of the airstrip, surveying the area with rifles in hand, they finally toss their weapons into their Jeep and zoom off into the growing gloom.

I heave a sigh, sit up, and begin pulling my shirt out of my waistband so I can get this annoying bag off my irritated skin.

"Well, *that* was fun," Bash drawls.

"The baboon shooting or the Crawl for Your Life event?"

"Both." He pushes himself to a sitting position and pulls a leaf from his hair.

The package of cosmetics slides out onto my thigh, the plastic slimy with sweat. The scratches on my back burn and itch even worse now. "Do you think Elaine called those soldiers?"

He shrugs.

Which pretty much sums up my attitude, too. There's no way to tell.

Where the hell is Aunt Penny? Was she stopped by those soldiers? Is she a prisoner, or worse? My anxiety is ratcheting up, and I have no paper bag to breathe into.

The sun has nearly set, and the nightly African bush concert is beginning. Heard from inside a hut, the roars and chuffing and trumpets of the wild are exotic and intriguing. Out here, they give me the shivers. I'm anxious to get back to that little terminal building. I hope we don't have to spend the night in there.

Bash is thinking the same thing. "Back to the shack?" He lays a hand on my thigh.

I place one foot on the ground and start to rise. Then, through the intertwined branches, I see a movement in the dim light. Something large, light-colored. Then the shape contracts and through the tall grass, two large golden eyes focus in our direction.

Twenty-Seven

*O*hgodohgodohgod. I slap a shaky hand on Bash's shoulder.

"What?"

"Lion," I whisper, although I'm not sure why it would make any difference to keep my voice low.

Another tawny shape moves behind Bash, and I know there's at least one more big cat only yards away.

Bash's eyes are round. His face goes rigid.

"Up!" I plead. "Climb. Now!"

Without waiting for his agreement, I grab the bag of cosmetics in my teeth and begin to scramble up the tree I was scoping out earlier. It's hard going, because the branches are so close together that it's hard to slither between them. Whatever type of tree this is, I hate it. But it's incredible how fast you can crawl through painful obstacles when you think that otherwise you might die. Spiky branches tear at my face and hair and snap as I push through them, showering Bash with sticks and bark until he manages to climb up to my level on the opposite side of the tree.

Unfortunately, these trees are dinky by my Pacific Northwest standards, and we have to stop when we're probably only about twenty-five feet from the ground. I release my grip on the plastic bag and set it down on the branch between my thighs. My jaws hurt from clenching the blasted thing. Bash and I are both breathing like we just raced ten miles at max speed.

Staring down through the thick branches, I can barely make out a big male lion sitting at the base of the tree, flanked by two females. As we watch, one of the females rises to her hind feet and stretches her paws up the trunk of our tree.

"Good thing lions can't climb," Bash says.

I hate to be the one to inform him. "That's a myth."

"Well, damn," he replies, for once accepting my expertise without question.

Fortunately, after clawing the trunk, the lioness sits back on her haunches and the feline trio watches us. The male licks his lips, which seems ominous, but then he lowers his belly to the ground. A radio collar is bolted around his neck, which diminishes his majesty. I wonder if it interferes with his daily lion life, making it harder to hunt or fight or eat.

"He's giving up," Bash says, sounding optimistic.

"It's mostly the females that hunt."

"Thanks for that note of cheer." He shifts position, showering leaves and bits of bark onto the lions below.

I watch as the females shake the bark from their heads. The male doesn't move, just lets the sticks and leaves rain onto his tawny coat like they're too insignificant to bother with.

"Poor guy."

"*Poor* guy?"

Although I can't see my partner's face from my current position, I'm sure Bash is raising an eyebrow right now. I know the lion's radio collar is for research and I should probably be praying that the scientists who placed it there will soon show up to check on their subject, but it's depressing how humans leave their ugly marks on everything they touch. "I wish we could take his collar off."

"While he wishes he could take our heads off."

The lionesses continue to study the two humans overhead, and unfortunately, their interest in us seems to be growing. It's getting so dark now that soon we won't be able to see the cats at all.

A few minutes later, we hear a lion scratch its claws again on the trunk below us.

"What do you think our odds are?" Bash asks.

What can I say that would sound encouraging? "I think we're in the right place. Baboons and other monkeys hide in trees overnight."

"And what do they do if a lion decides to climb up?"

"Uh... they usually jump to the next tree."

We both look at the nearest tree, which is a good thirty feet away. And also irrelevant, since we inept humans couldn't jump from tree to tree even if a lion was about to snag us.

Then we hear branches cracking below.

A lion *is* about to snag us.

Twenty-Eight

"Shit!" Bash and I yell simultaneously. It's hard to be eloquent when you're on the verge of being eaten.

It will be interesting to find out what happens next when they make the movie version of this incident. Fortunately, in real life, we hear a vehicle heading our way. A second later, headlights rake across the airstrip, briefly illuminating one lion in the lower branches, as well as two—no, three—more on the ground. Then the lights move away, and we hear the vehicle skid to a stop in the gravel before reaching the terminal shack. Next, the vehicle backs up, the headlights swing our way, and the vehicle starts bouncing through the tall grass, heading for our position.

The three lions on the ground grunt and dash into the darkness. The lioness in the tree twists her body into a pretzel, then drops to the ground and races away after her companions.

I can't make up my mind whether to be relieved or even more panicked. Is it better to be eaten by a predator or shot by thugs? I have just decided that I'd rather be a lion dinner, part of the circle of life, which is at least useful in the grand scheme of things, when a female voice below shouts "Tana? Sebastian?"

Penny. Oh, thank you, whatever-is-in-control-of-the-universe-if-anything-is.

"Tana?" I can see a pale outline of my aunt's face illuminated by dashboard lights as she cracks open the door of the Jeep and sticks her head out.

"Coming!" I yell, as if she's summoning us to the dinner table. I tuck in my shirt again and stuff the cosmetics bag inside for the descent. It's no easier than the ascent, with small twigs giving way under our feet as we squeeze downward inside the network of branches.

When Bash and I reach the ground, my aunt gives me a quick, awkward hug. "Sorry to be so late." She glances from me to Bash and back again. "All okay here?"

She doesn't even bother to mention the lions. Was this sort of thing a normal part of growing up in Zimbabwe? Did my mother often get treed by lions?

"I had to drive Elaine to the quarantine site," she explains, "and then we both had to be inoculated with the new vaccine, and then I had to take her to town and pick up a shipment of food for camp and take that back."

"Did Elaine call or text anyone?" Bash asks.

Penny turns to him. "I can't say whether she communicated with anyone. We weren't together all the time."

He tells her about the soldiers. Her face goes stiff, and her lips form the word *shite* although she doesn't say it aloud. A frown lingers on her face.

"Did she hand the orange bag off to anyone?" I ask.

"She still had it with her when I dropped her off at the hotel."

"Any idea where she's going next?"

It would be nice to follow that orange bag to see what Elaine does with it, but Penny shakes her head. "When I next get the chance, I'll ask the driver who works for the hotel."

Then we hear rustling sounds from the dark bushes off to the side where the headlight beams don't reach, and our three heads swivel in that direction.

"Best get in," she suggests.

I take the front seat and slide the bag of cosmetics up onto the dash.

"Did you open that bag?"

I'm insulted. "No. We're not stupid."

"Good."

"Besides, we were a little busy, what with the soldier and the lions…"

"What did the containers look like under the scanner?"

"Uh." I passed the bag under the scanner, but I didn't really study the image on the screen. I glance at Bash in the back seat. He presses his lips together and frowns, which tells me he's also embarrassed that neither of us thought of that.

"I was distracted, making the switch," I admit.

"Okay then." Penny stops at the shed.

Knowing lions are roaming nearby, I'm not eager to get out of the Jeep, but my aunt jumps out and enters the building without a second thought, flinging on the light switch inside the door and then powering on the scanner. "We need to hurry."

After the machine warms up, she passes the cosmetics bag inside and we all stare at the screen. The contents of the bags look pretty much the same inside as they do outside. Filled with solid goop that may or may not be lipstick and lotions. "Not gold dust," she concludes. "Nor diamonds."

"Drugs?" I suggest.

"Possibly." She shuts down the machine. "Or possibly it's just lipstick and lotions and such." She gives me a skeptical look before she bends down and unplugs the scanner.

Now I feel like I may have risked all our lives for nothing.

Bash unzips the orange bag. "Then let's check it out."

Penny slaps a hand on top of his. "Stop, Sebastian. We have no idea what may be in there. Poison is a frequent weapon between tribes in Africa."

He jerks his hands away.

"I'll take these containers to be tested in Jo'burg after we get back." My aunt zips the bag again. She hands it to me, but now I don't want to hold it, either. I clutch one corner of the bag with two fingertips.

"Heave-ho, team," my aunt says. "We've got to move that scanner."

Heave-ho? I want to shower, and eat, and sleep, in that order. I don't want to heft heavy equipment around.

"Those soldiers may be back later to see if anyone shows up to claim it. And even in Zimbabwe police can match fingerprints."

That does it. It takes all three of us to shove the scanner

machine into the back of the Jeep. Fortunately it separates into three pieces. Bash has to share the back seat with the scanner part. Penny then hurtles down the dirt road, and we all bounce around inside, clinging to whatever is within reach.

"Wouldn't want to be caught here," she apologizes. "And off with the uniforms. T-shirts on the floor in back, Sebastian."

He finds them and hands me one, and I peel out of my uniform shirt and pull the tee over my head. Bash does the same in the back seat.

"Are we flying out tonight?" I'm not sure exactly where we flew into yesterday, but it wasn't too far away.

She shakes her head. "After sunset, that would be too suspicious; the government would assume we're running drugs. Dawn, tomorrow."

Pairs of glowing eyes reflect our headlights from the tall grass at the sides of the road. "More lions?" I ask.

Penny's gaze flicks briefly to the side and back. "Could be a few. More likely springhares."

I'd like to see those kangaroo-like creatures, but I guess this is not the time. Penny takes a sharp right and soon hurtles into a clearing in what looks like a resort area set among the trees. Several cabins and a lodge, plus small outbuildings of various sizes form a small compound. No lights are on inside the buildings. We sit there a minute, headlights illuminating the Houston Hunt Club sign over the front porch of the lodge.

"As in Houston, Texas?" I ask.

"Yes, Yanks." she says. "Good. No one seems to be in residence now." She maneuvers the Jeep over to a small outbuilding.

"What do they hunt?"

"The Big Five," she replies. This is a common term used by game lodges to indicate lion, leopard, elephant, rhino, Cape buffalo—the five animals hunters throughout history have most wanted to shoot in Africa. "It's big business here."

I can't help thinking about how Bailey would have ended up as a high-priced target on a game ranch in Texas if Bash and I hadn't won the Verde Island race. I miss my elephant so much. If everything goes according to plan, I should be back home in three days. Sabrina and Aaron will still be pissed at me and Emilio will still be jealous, but I'll smooth that over eventually. The hunger to see my home and family wars with my physical hunger after not eating all day. When my stomach growls in protest, I rub my hand against my belly.

There's a combination lock on the door of the outbuilding. Penny extracts a pry bar from the rear of the Jeep, thrusts it through the U-shaped lock bar, and leans on the pry handle until the lock cracks in two. It looks like she's performed the maneuver before.

"You didn't see that." She pulls open the door.

"See what?" Bash responds.

We unload the scanner into the shed, alongside an ATV with flat tires and a rusting gas-powered generator. And then we hop in the Jeep and take off again.

"Won't the scanner get stolen?" I ask, clinging to the dash as we race down the road.

She makes a huffing noise. "Stealing from big spenders like the Houston Hunt Club could mean a death sentence in

Zimbabwe. I'll arrange for pickup soon. But if it happens to be found, no government lackey would question the Yanks about what they might be doing with it."

I wrestle with this idea for a while, trying to decide if this hands-off policy indicates international diplomacy or multinational corruption or just good-ol'-boy business as usual.

Penny drops us off at a different house than we stayed at last night, this one a remote farm house. She introduces us as MSF camp laborers, which fits with our disheveled appearance, and she asks the housekeeper to feed and keep us until dawn, when she'll be back to pick us up.

Understandably, our hostess asks us to shower before dinner. The soapy water is painful on the scratches across my back and sides, but I don't want to call attention to those by asking for ointment. After a hearty meal of stew and biscuits and lemonade, Bash and I fall into bed.

"We escaped from lions," Bash murmurs.

"Not to mention soldiers with guns," I counter.

"I made some money, too. That wad of cash Elaine handed me is worth nearly fifty bucks."

We both laugh. Elaine has to be so frustrated that her bribe didn't work.

"I sincerely hope tomorrow will be much more boring," he says.

"I second that."

Twenty-Nine

The next day, we haven't been back in Jo'burg for more than a half hour when my cell bleeps at me. I glance at it, expecting Aaron or Sabrina or even my colleagues at the zoo, but the screen says CLASSIFIED.

I answer with some trepidation. "Hello?"

"Hold for the former President of the United States," a female voice says.

WTF? Those few words launch my nerves into outer space. I stand up at attention, stare at the phone, glance around in panic for Bash. I'm on the patio by myself; everyone else is in the house.

"Miss Grey." In two words, Garrison manages to convey that he is irate. I'm surprised smoke isn't shooting out of this phone.

I can't think of anything to say.

"What are you dragging my boy into? You have no idea what you're messing around with. I could have you charged with treason."

Treason? The former president of the United States is calling to accuse me of treason? What is he talking about? I am speechless with terror. I'm so glad this isn't a videochat.

After a few seconds of silence between us, his tone softens a little. "I know you are very young, so I'm sure you do not understand the subtleties of international diplomacy. Our relations with Zimbabwe are delicate. I suggest you immediately fly back to your little wildlife preserve in Washington State and return to your cozy little dung-moving job at the zoo. For the safety of all concerned. Do not involve Sebastian in any of your insane schemes. Discontinue your relationship with him. You need to get this all under control. For the safety of all concerned. Do you hear me?"

This at least, is a question I can answer. "Yes, sir."

Then the call abruptly ends, and a photo pops onto my cell screen. It's me and Bash in our fake uniforms, at the scanner in Zimbabwe. The photo Elaine took yesterday.

What the hell? How did that photo end up in Garrison's hands? And how did it get there so fast? Does Elaine have a direct line to Garrison? I'm shaking. *For the safety of all concerned.* What does he mean by that? He said it twice. He knows where I live and where I work. Does *all concerned* include everyone I know?

The patio door slides open behind me. Bash sticks his head out, his hair still wet from the shower. "Dinner in ten," he announces. Then, seeing my expression, the tranquil expression falls from his face, and he steps outside and closes the door behind him. "What's up, Tana?"

"Nothing." I shove the cell phone into my back pocket.

"I can see you're upset."

"Uh...it's just Bailey," I lie.

"Is he sick?"

I manufacture a convincing detail. "Just trying one of his escape attempts. I've got to get home as soon as possible."

He puts an arm around my shoulders. "You'll be there within forty-eight hours."

"Yeah." I swallow. "I just hope the house is still standing and Sabrina's still talking to me."

I take a deep breath, try to push Garrison's threats from my mind, but of course that's all I can think of. "Heard anything recently from your Bio-Pop?"

Bash gives me a curious look. "He sent congratulations after the race. And then a rebuke a couple of days ago about ditching the Secret Service."

Now that I think about it, I'm surprised that we haven't been tracked down. I always keep the GPS function on my phone turned off, and Bash usually does, too. But it seems like the Secret Service could still do some fancy triangulation or other hocus-pocus to find us. Suddenly I'm worried about Grand and Penny and Marianne; would they be part of *all concerned*?

I don't know what to think now. I want to talk to someone more knowledgeable than I am, but I don't have a clue who that would be.

Bash is still studying my face. "Why did you ask about Garrison?"

"No particular reason." I want to tell him, but I'm not sure I should. After dithering for a minute, I mutter, "There better be wine," and precede him into the house.

"Did you enjoy your tour of the MSF facilities?" Grand wants to know at dinner. "I hope Penny was careful." We didn't choose to enlighten my grandfather or Marianne about our plan to intercept the QTL courier.

"Father!" Penny scolds. "Of course I didn't take them to the quarantine area."

"We were impressed," I tell him. My brain clicks through the events—the scanner, Elaine, the switch of the cosmetics, the soldiers, the guns, trying to fix on some detail I can share. The lions. I add, "And last night we saw lions."

"Oh ho!" His eyes gleam. "Now *that's* the Zimbabwe I remember. You can never be too careful when walking after dark in the bush."

"Got that right," Bash says.

"What's next?" Marianne asks. "How long can you stay?"

I glance at my aunt. "Well, tomorrow morning we promised Penny to help with an MSF problem, and then in the evening, Sebastian and I have to fly back to the States."

Grand regards Penny with concern. "What sort of problem is MSF having?"

There's an awkward moment of indecision where a little zing of electricity ricochets between Bash, Penny, and me.

Bash is the first to recover. "Nothing major." He waves his hand in the air over his roast beef. "It's a fairly common issue of software incompatibility that can be fixed by uninstalling one plug-in and downloading a couple of security patches."

His tech talk has the intended effect of shutting us all up.

In actuality, we are waiting for the report from the private testing lab where Penny dropped off the containers on our way back from the airport. If the containers turn out to hold only lipstick and lotions, I'll feel like a fool, but I'll be so relieved. Except that then I'd be back to square one, with no reason for my parents' murders.

Unfortunately, the lab results are not delivered until moments before we have to leave, and Penny tells us she will wait until we are parked at the airport to enlighten us. Her face is taut with anxiety. I barely slept last night, thinking about Garrison's phone call, and the suspense that Penny insists on is jangling my nerves. During the drive, I try to distract myself by studying my cell phone. Wordage gives me *pervicacious*, which means *stubborn, dogged, willful*. Geographastic informs me that Cape Verde—or Cabo Verde—is a Portuguese island nation in the Atlantic, west of Senegal. I wonder if our plane will pass over those islands today.

After running into several traffic jams that have no obvious cause, we finally arrive at the Johannesburg airport.

As soon as we've pulled up to the curb, Bash orders my aunt, "Spill it, Penny."

"The cosmetic containers were full of opiates," I guess.

In the U.S., there's an opiate crisis that is lucrative for the drug manufacturers but is killing off thousands of people. I'm guessing that could be just as true in Africa, and Quarrel Tayson is in the perfect position to pull that off on an international level. The pharma industry is a major supporter of Garrison's political party, and I'd be surprised if he didn't have major investments there, too. Like Bash reminded me, Quarrel Tayson Corporation has its greedy fingers into almost everything. Do they own Bash's Bio-Pop, too?

Next, my thoughts flash to Elizabeth Abbott and that selfie. "Were opiates mixed into that lipstick?" Did Liz die of an overdose? Or was it something else? My second guess: "Some other kind of poison?"

"Not opiates." Penny shakes her head. "Not poison." After a brief pause, she adds, "Well, poison of a sort."

I can't stand it. I'm ready to shake *her*. "What?"

Suddenly I don't want her to tell Bash because he's safer if he doesn't know. I hold up a hand. "Wait—don't tell Sebastian!"

His eyes blaze. "What the hell, Tana?"

It's better for him to be furious at me than in danger. If I'm going to be charged with treason, he doesn't deserve to go down with me. It's better *for the safety of all concerned* if he doesn't know. "It's not your fight, Bash. Penny and I are family, this is our history—"

"Penny." He crosses his arms and stares her down. "What was in the cosmetic containers?"

My aunt takes a deep breath and then says, "Ebola."

"What?!" Bash frowns. "Why would QT be importing Ebola when they are constantly sending vaccines to stop it?"

My thoughts stop buzzing around like fruit flies and zero in the target.

Omigod.

Omigod.

Oh my God.

Finally, everything I've learned over the years makes perfect sense.

"They're eradicating the last strain of Ebola while importing the next strain." My voice is grim. "Genetic engineering."

My mother specialized in that. *It's not only unethical, it's immoral.* This has to be what she meant. How could I have missed this?

It's a consistent revenue stream. My father realized the connection, too. What better source of income could any corporation manufacture than to create diseases for which only it had the vaccines?

Liz Abbott spread death over her lips when she tried on the lipstick from the *orange bag* in Senegal. Quarrel Tayson realized that she was infected, and killed her before she reached the contagious stage. She probably shared the cosmetics with her friend there, and that's why the next outbreak was in Senegal.

Bash is stunned into silence for a long moment, then says, "I need to see that spreadsheet again, Tana."

I can see it so clearly now. The QTL rep simply transports the contaminated cosmetics in the orange bag to a new area and then leaves them in strategic locations. In poor countries, of course the lotions and lipstick would be eagerly grabbed up by the locals. Who would ever suspect Ebola in skin lotion? I'm so glad we didn't touch those containers.

A virus that can be quickly mutated in a state-of-the-art lab. Appropriate samples delivered to the CDC to show the new strains of the virulent virus. A never-ending revenue stream.

I've been injected dozens of times with QTL vaccines before traveling to Third World countries for endurance races. Military forces around the world are routinely immunized. Employees of NGOs. Travelers. State Department staff. Airline crews. The list of customers is endless. Unethical and immoral indeed.

I turn to Penny. "Where was Elaine going after she left the camp in Zimbabwe?"

"Rwanda."

Bash frowns. "So QT will expect the next outbreak to be in Rwanda."

And what will happen when that outbreak doesn't occur?

Elaine from QTL has that photo of Bash and me with the scanner. So does the former U.S. President. Is Garrison part of all this? Does he already suspect that his son and I stole the tainted cosmetics?

It won't take long for QTL to figure out what happened to the latest strain of Ebola. And then what? Will Bash and I die on the side of the road in a convenient accident like Liz Abbott?

"What now?" I ask my aunt.

"I've already arranged for someone in Rwanda to follow Elaine. With luck, my girl there will get more evidence." She tucks a strand of hair behind her ear. "And I'll hire someone to follow the next rep who receives shipments. That shouldn't be too difficult."

You can't say that my aunt isn't brave. And pervicacious. And maybe, just maybe, Elaine and Garrison and whoever is behind this conspiracy at QTL won't realize that Penny knows. She wasn't in the photo; she was just Elaine's driver on that day, and her last name is no longer Patterson.

"You're going to miss your plane," she reminds us.

We all step out of the car to say goodbye. Bash opens the trunk to get our luggage.

I can't stop staring at my aunt's face. I'm terrified about what might happen to her. "Oh, Penny, I'm so sorry I involved you."

She takes my shoulders in her strong hands, pulls me into a tight hug, and says in a harsh whisper, "You listen to me, Tana-Amelia. Piper was my *sister*. My *identical twin*. I want to do this. I *have* to do this."

Tears run down my face, and my throat is so tight I can't speak. When she finally lets go, I feel like I'm stumbling away from a car wreck.

Bash's expression looks as if he might be experiencing internal injuries, too. God only knows what his quick brain is piecing together now.

"I should never have told you about the test results," Penny mourns, clasping her hands over mine. "You two will never get through security with those faces."

Bash straightens his shoulders, combs his fingers through his hair. "We'll cope."

"At least you'll be safer in the States," Penny says.

Why would she think that? The U.S. is where this threat comes from. And if Garrison is involved ... but I didn't tell Penny about that photo coming back to me like a malevolent boomerang.

"We'll figure it out." Bash slaps me gently on the shoulder. "C'mon, Tana."

"We will figure it out," Penny leans forward to repeat into my ear.

"Stay safe," I breathe into hers. "I love you ..." I almost say Mom, but I change it at the last second to "Penny."

"And you, too, sweetheart. I will come meet Aaron as soon as you say."

I hug her again, even harder this time. "Thanks for everything."

I don't want to let go of her. I may never see my Mom Lookalike again. She helped me find the answers to my questions. But now I realize that although I have the answers, I have no solutions, and we are all in danger.

I wipe away my tears and tackle airport security with Bash. All the way back to New York City, I fantasize about our jet exploding, the pieces raining down into the sea. But then I realize that only lotion and lipstick are being spread around Rwanda, so it won't happen yet. Quarrel Tayson has to wait out the incubation period, and then they'll be perplexed about why Ebola isn't breaking out in that country as planned.

So it could be a month or even two before they suspect anything is wrong.

Except...damn Elaine. They might never have connected any of us to this if she hadn't snapped that damn photo. Garrison has it. How many others?

Quarrel Tayson killed Liz Abbott because they realized she had contaminated herself with Ebola. She probably never even knew what had happened. I hope she was happy after her adventure to Casablanca and her secret side trip to Senegal to see her friend. I hope she died on impact in that hit-and-run.

What horrible hopes to have.

I wonder how many days Sebastian Callendro and Tanzania Grey have left on this planet.

Thirty

Knowledge is power, and that's why they've let me live: in the past, they realized I didn't have either. Up to now, it was clear I didn't know anything. Now, my knowledge could be deadly. *To all concerned.*

Bash, sitting beside me, is clearly in shock. We're afraid to talk out loud, so we are texting each other. Several times now, he has written something along the lines of *Maybe it was a mistake, Tana* and *Accidental contamination?"*

Each time I write back *No mistake.*

I know Bash is having a hard time wrapping his head around the idea that a major American corporation could be willing to kill people for profit. Sebastian Callendro may be jaded about politics, but he doesn't share my history of murder and cover-up and threatening pursuers. Quarrel Tayson Corporation has supported his Bio-Pop's political career, and more recently, Bash's own projects and his racing hobby. The corporation was awarded the Presidential Medal of Freedom for all the lives saved by the vaccines.

And lives *were* saved. My mother ended Ebola while working at Quarrel Tayson Laboratories. She was simply too naïve to ever predict that conquering Ebola would end her life, too. My dad probably spotted the pattern in the spreadsheets and suggested what QTL was up to. And based on what I now know about Piper Amy Patterson's history, she'd be determined to reveal the truth.

A sob threatens to erupt from my throat. I clap a hand over my mouth to keep it in.

Another text from Bash leaps onto my cell phone screen. *Can't be real. It's too big.*

Finally, I pull up Elaine's photo of us at the scanner, the one that Garrison sent me. Nudging Bash with my elbow, I shove the phone into his lap. His fingers close over mine and he pulls the phone closer, studying the photo. I run a finger along the conversation ID line. *TLGarrison.*

He turns to me, his eyes huge.

I pull back my phone and type Called me yesterday. Told me I'd better leave you alone and go back to my manure-shoveling job 'for the safety of all concerned.'

After Bash reads that, he stares at the seat back in front of him for a long moment. Then he finally turns to me and whispers, "What now?"

I shake my head. And then I lean over to show him as I press an icon on my phone.

Delete conversation? a popup asks. I tap Yes.

He does the same thing on his phone, and we both put our cells away. All around us, most passengers are sleeping. A few flight attendants are awake, quietly cruising the aisles. I turn my face to the window and watch the clouds below. We are flying above a thick cloud layer that looks like a field of snow. Stars twinkle all around us in the dark heavens. It's beautiful up here.

I keep thinking about Mom and Dad. Aaron. And then Penny and Grand and Marianne. Grandma Laura, whom I never got to meet. Mom's colleague in Zimbabwe—Gambel? Elizabeth Abbott. Everything all these people went through. All for the sake of power and profits?

A moan startles me, especially after I realize that sound came from my throat. I massage my larynx with my fingers and try to focus on something else.

Bash elbows me, and when I turn away from the window, he thunks two little airplane bottles of wine down onto my tray, along with a plastic cup. He's already emptied one of his bottles into his cup, and he lifts that in a silent toast.

I pour a bottle into my cup and hold it with my right hand as I slip my left into Bash's, interlacing my fingers with his. What the hell are we going to do? What *can* we do? What's going to happen now?

Somehow, after we both finish off our second bottle of wine, sleep finally comes.

Thirty-One

In New York, Bash and I have to part company. He's off to Albuquerque to finish the waste treatment and recycling center he's been building there with volunteers, and I have to go back to my home in Western Washington, to Sabrina and Aaron and Bailey and to my cozy little dung-shoveling job at the zoo. I'm actually looking forward to wielding my shovel and wheelbarrow again; I need physical labor right now to tamp down my mental anguish.

At his departure gate, I don't want to let go of Sebastian Callendro. This is the second time we've been through life-threatening and life-altering experiences together. I can hardly believe we've been gone from home for only two weeks. The world has changed in that time. At least *my* world has; and I worry that I have dragged Bash off the precipice of his comfortable existence into the dangerous abyss of my own. I pray that his status as Garrison's son will protect him.

I can't imagine how I will protect myself. Could I invent a new, third persona? I might be able to pull that off for myself, but it would be nearly impossible to move an elephant and a fourteen-year-old boy to a new location and find a new job. Not many employers are willing to take a chance on an almost-nineteen-year-old with only a GED and Habitat Maintenance experience.

As I say goodbye to Bash, I am painfully aware that this may be the last time I see him. When the powers that be piece our activities together, they will find a way to slap me in prison, or—more likely—arrange for an 'accident.' People die in auto collisions every day. I usually commute to the zoo by bicycle, and that offers the opportunity for an even less suspicious fatality.

The airline calls for Bash's boarding group. He turns to me, pulls an object from his hip pocket, and hands me a cell phone. "Here."

I stare at it. It's not his; not mine. This one is cheap and blue.

"Prepaid," he says, then taps his chest pocket. "Mine's right here. I bought them in the gift shop while you were in the restroom. I already put my number in yours, and yours in mine."

I'm relieved that he plans to stay in touch. "Thanks."

"These are untraceable. I used cash. The clerk didn't recognize me."

I'd hardly recognize him myself if I hadn't spent the last two weeks with him. His beard has grown out to what might be a fashionable length in some circles or simply considered unkempt in others. He's wearing eyeglasses with clear lenses that he donned at the Johannesburg airport, explaining that they make it easier for The President's Son to travel incognito.

"Stay safe," is the last thing I say to him.

"Tana," he murmurs, putting his arms around me. "I..."

Then he pulls me in close and gives me a kiss. Not a quick peck like we've exchanged before, congratulating each other during races, but a mind-blowing, whisker-rasping, tongue-exploring kiss. A man standing nearby actually claps as Bash pulls back, shoots me a tentative smile, and then vanishes through the departure gate.

As I stare at the door through which he has walked, I am breathless. What did *that* mean? Does he, too, realize that Tanzania Grey might not be in this world much longer? Was that a final goodbye kiss, or—? I helped him disappear once. Maybe he's planning to disappear again.

But he gave me the phone. Which means he wants to call me at least once more. Or wants me to call him. I zip it carefully into my backpack.

The intercom announces the final call for my Seattle flight, and I have to jog to another concourse, with airport security scrutinizing me every step of the way.

The flight from New York to Seattle is the usual cramped cross-U.S. torture. From Wordage, I learn *venal–open to bribery*, and *salient–significant, prominent*. Geographastic teaches me that the New Madrid Seismic Zone, which runs under parts of Arkansas, Missouri, Tennessee, Kentucky, and Illinois, once fractured so badly that the Mississippi River ran backwards for several hours. Wow, when did that happen? There's no date listed. We have a lot of faults and a lot of rivers in western Washington. Do I need to add fractured faults to my list of things to worry about?

I even try to do some math problems, but with everything

that's happened, I can't make my mind focus on geometry; my thoughts go round and round in an endless spin cycle. By the time I deplane, every muscle in my body hurts, and I'm ravenous. But I still have hours to go before I reach home—rapid transit to downtown Seattle, Amtrak to my stop an hour north of town, then a couple of busses out into the countryside, and finally about an hour's walk. After looking at my watch, I realize with despair that that last hour's walk will be in the dark.

An excellent opportunity for a hit-and-run.

I'm trotting for the airport exit, wearing my backpack, pulling my carry-on, when I hear my name. "Tana!"

I'm not expecting anyone. Probably Tanya, not Tana.

"Tanzania Grey!" A hand clamps onto my shoulder.

I jump about a foot in the air, dropping my suitcase handle as I whirl around, ready to fight off the attacker.

A handsome dark-haired man in Army uniform stands in front of me. Emilio scoops me into his arms. "Welcome home, Tana!"

And then he plants a kiss on my lips, every bit as passionate and lingering as Bash's. *Whoa.*

When we come up for air, I ask, "What are you doing here, Shadow?"

His dark eyes cloud. Or at least his real eye does, the fake one always looks the same. "Can't I give my girl a ride?"

"But you're stationed in California."

He shrugs. "Weekend leave. I have to be back on Monday, but I couldn't wait to see you, so I came up. I rented a car." He brushes a strand of hair out of my face, and then pulls my slipping backpack strap up onto my shoulder. "Aren't you glad to see me?"

Confused might be a better adjective for what I'm feeling right now, but after my wild imaginings, I'm thrilled to see a friendly face. "You wouldn't believe how glad I am to see you, Shadow!"

I give him another quick kiss to emphasize that. "I was so focused on making the rapid transit. You surprised me."

His expression softens, and he bends down and picks up the handle of my carry-on from the floor. "I'm glad I can still do that. You surprise *me* all the time. Like right now. I barely recognized you. What happened to your hair?"

I put my hand up to pat my new 'do, layered and only barely shoulder length now. I'm going to have a hard time pinning it up at the zoo. "Some of it got burned off, so I had to get it cut in Johannesburg."

Frown lines crease his forehead. "*Burned* off?"

Of course he wouldn't know. The Extreme African Endurance Challenge was not broadcast on any TV sports channel. I wonder if the Zimbabweans will put that summary vid on YouTube. After removing the clip added by Lyman and Pratt, of course.

I chuckle at Emilio's perplexed expression. "We have a lot to talk about."

"Yes, we do." Taking my hand, he pulls me toward the parking lot.

Even with a car, it takes over ninety minutes to get to WildRun, my country home, and the sun is setting as we pull up to the gate and key in the security code. As we cruise up the driveway to the house, a gigantic beast barrels out of the dark, running after the car, startling me. Then I remember Sabrina mentioned that Bailey destroyed the wooden fence that separated his domain from our farmhouse.

Bailey won't recognize this rental car. To him, it's an unwelcome intruder in his territory.

I leap out as soon as the car slows. My elephant slams to a stop beside me and trumpets so loudly it nearly blows out my eardrums.

"Bailey." I stretch out my hand toward him. "I'm happy to see you."

He hooks his trunk around my neck and jerks me into his front leg, then rubs me down with his lower jaw and trunk, flapping his ears around my shoulders. This is a much rougher greeting than usual. His exuberance proves my elephant really missed me. I lean against him, patting his shoulder, caressing his ear until he relaxes a little. Then I take a couple of steps back, but his trunk immediately wraps around my waist and I have to return. This time I lean against his broad forehead as I stroke him. He rumbles, either complaining about my absence or welcoming me home.

Sabrina and Aaron and Emilio stand on the front porch, laughing. Finally, after my clothes are thoroughly filthy and I smell like a fellow elephant, Bailey decides he can let me go. I even have snot in my hair.

Still, my brother hugs me. "We have pizza. And salad. Sabrina made me wait."

"Well, now we can all eat." I hold out my arms to my housemate for a hug. "Thanks, Sabrina."

She laughs and backs up a step. "No way!"

I look down at my clothes. Bailey must have been rolling in dirt or possibly even manure before he greeted me. I'm streaked with filth. "I think I may take a quick shower first."

"Excellent idea," Sabrina says. "And Aaron, go change your shirt and wash your hands."

My brother races to beat me to our one bathroom.

It's great to be home. I missed my bed, my elephant, my cats, and even the goats. I even missed my job. I will appreciate all these things more now that I realize they could be taken from me in an instant.

It feels weird to have Shadow with us again. He recuperated here for months after his injuries last year. He was sort of our third housemate, before Aaron arrived. But now that there are two males in the house, my brother is always trying to compete with Emilio. Aaron talks about how far he can throw rocks. Emilio doesn't help when he starts telling Aaron about all the weapons he handled overseas.

Finally, when Aaron brags, "I stabbed two people," I have to call a halt to the macho weenie wagging.

"That part of your history is nothing to be proud of, Aaron," I remind my brother. Turning to Emilio, I say, "Grow up, Shadow."

Emilio is acting oddly, alternately throwing his arm around me and then taunting me in some way. Or maybe it's just my imagination. I excuse myself to crash early, citing my jet lag and the fact that I have to work the early shift at the zoo tomorrow.

"But tomorrow's Saturday," Emilio protests. "And I'm here."

"The animals don't take weekends off. And I have to pay back all the people who worked in my place while I was in Africa."

"Oh yes," he says, glowering. "Africa. Racing with the Golden Boy."

I sigh. Will I always have to deal with his jealousy?

Thirty-Two

At the zoo the next day, it's actually soothing to wield my wheelbarrow and shovel. I work overtime and don't return home until after dark, feeling slightly guilty at the late hour, because Emilio is with us. I should be eager to get home to him, shouldn't I?

After saying hello to Bailey and giving him and the goats a pile of hay, I go into the house to find Emilio and Sabrina laughing together as they cook sloppy joes.

I inhale deeply, savoring the scent. "That smells great."

Sabrina leans against the cabinets and smiles toward Shadow. "Emilio's a good cook."

"She's just being modest." He wraps an arm around my housemate and pulls her in close. "It's all Sabrina."

Now I'm confused, and I excuse myself to shower and change clothes. As Emilio recuperated here last year, even though he was supposedly my fiancé, I suspected that he and Sabrina were attracted to each other. Then, after he nearly strangled her during one of his PTSD flashbacks, their teasing and touching ended.

At least I thought it had ended. Are he and I supposed to be engaged now, or is he again my adopted relative from Marisela's household, or what? Does he want me, or does he want Sabrina?

I long for the simplicity of running a race each day, of sleeping exhausted next to Bash. I don't know how to act in my own house anymore.

From the folds of an extra blanket on my closet shelf, I dig out that prepaid cell phone Bash gave me. There are texts from both Penny and Bash. Penny's message, sent hours ago, has a vid attached, and I watch rough cuts of Elaine doing exactly what we suspected. First, she's in a restroom somewhere, probably an airport or bus station in Rwanda. The lighting is poor and this seems to have been filmed through a slit that's probably around a toilet stall door.

A cleaning lady mops the floor behind Elaine as she checks her appearance in the mirror, cosmetics laid out on the counter in front of her. She powders her nose with a compact she takes from her purse, then stuffs the cosmetics back inside the orange bag, leaving the lipstick behind when she exits the room. After a quick glance around to make sure nobody's watching, the cleaning lady scoops up the lipstick and drops it in her pocket.

Next, there's a clip of Elaine in a market. She 'accidentally' drops a bottle of lotion while rummaging through her purse, and then, in a restaurant in the evening, she discards a tiny container of sunscreen under her napkin.

We've got them, Penny wrote in the accompanying text.

Now what?

What now? Bash echoes, typing in real time.

Like *I'm* supposed to know?

Is that enough evidence? I respond to both. And then, to Bash alone, *Heard from TLG?*

He texts back *No word* almost immediately. Nothing comes from Penny, but she's most likely asleep right now. I hide the phone, share dinner with my family, and hit the sheets so I can get up early for work again.

In the morning, I find a text from Penny saying she'll try to intercept the next shipment of vaccines from QTL to MSF, which is due to arrive in southern Zambia in a few days, to protect against the Zimbabwean strain leaking over the border. If the courier again brings a bag of Ebola-laden cosmetics and Penny can intercept it, we'll have all the proof we need. Salient proof. Or is that an oxymoron?

I'm terrified for Penny's safety, and using my secret phone, I close myself into my bedroom closet and call to tell her that. She assures me that she can bribe a servant or camp guard to switch the cosmetics this time. Apparently, sometimes it can be useful to live in a venal society.

Then I hide the phone again and ride my bike to the zoo. Dawn is breaking just as I pass through the employee entrance.

Yesterday, my first full day back, the routine of house and work and Aaron was comforting. Even though it was a bit awkward, it was nice to have Emilio with us, too. Today, only one day later, normal life is already starting to feel trivial. That's the way it always is after an extreme race; average days don't seem exciting enough. Plus, knowing what I know now,

I'm waiting for something big and truly horrible to happen. I wish I could see what Penny is doing half a world away.

Sunday evening, we have just enough time to have dinner together again and play a card game before we all start preparing for bed. Aaron's already in his room; he has school in the morning. Emilio has to get up in the wee hours to drive the car to the airport in Seattle and fly back to California, and I have to go back to work. Sabrina's letting me take her pickup, though, for which I'm grateful. It means another half hour of sleep for me, plus I can pick up Aaron after school so he won't have to ride the bus.

As I'm tucking in a blanket on the couch for Emilio and Sabrina's looking through the clutter in the living room for her truck keys, Emilio says, "Wait a minute, you two. I have to tell you something."

Sabrina and I stop what we're doing to look at him. He may be a wounded warrior now, but he's still as handsome as ever. Smooth olive skin with a darker shade of black whiskers along his jaw, ebony hair with just a hint of curl, even when it's as short as it is now, eyes so dark they're almost black, even if one of them is not exactly zeroing in on me now. Dark, smoldering. My Shadow.

His face contorts as he debates what to say, and then he swoops over to me and wraps me in a hug. "Tana." He releases me, strides swiftly to Sabrina and gives her a brief hug, too. "Sabrina."

Then he positions himself a little apart from both me and Sabrina, putting his arms behind him and spreading his legs like he's assuming the military 'at ease' position, which never looks particularly easy to me.

After taking a deep breath, he moves his hands forward, sliding them into his front pockets, and announces, "I've met someone."

No wonder Emilio has been acting so strangely.

He doesn't want me *or* Sabrina any more.

The three of us share an awkward moment of silence.

Shadow and I could never have worked as husband and wife, I tell myself. I swallow and then lick my lips to wet them. "Is she a soldier, too?"

"Yeah. She's a helicopter mechanic like me." He eagerly pulls his cell phone out of his pocket. The picture he brings up shows a young woman with short dark curls and flashing black eyes. In the photo, she has a wrench in her hand and a smudge of dirt on her cheek, but she's laughing. She's not especially pretty, but there's something about her smile that's magnetic. "Her name is Lilia. Lilia Martinez."

The way he smiles at her picture and the syrupy tone of his voice tells me this is real. I check Sabrina's expression. Her posture is tense, her gaze still focused on Lilia's photo.

"Lilia doesn't mind about this." Emilio slaps a hand against the damaged leg that causes his limp, and then he points at his right eye. "Or this."

I want to tell him that I never counted his injuries against him either, but I know it haunts him that he can no longer run with me and that he has only one functional eye.

I put a hand on his wrist. "I'm happy for you, Shadow."

His gaze meets mine. "Really?"

"Really. You deserve to be happy. Lilia looks nice. I can't

wait to meet her."

He glances toward Sabrina. My housemate's smile is stiff, but she immediately nods and says, "I'm happy for you, too, Emilio."

Despite our reassurances, I know his revelation wounds both of us. I could never see beyond our future wedding day, but I don't want to lose Emilio Santos. He's seen me at my worst, when I was a scared, starving, stupid fourteen-year-old. He held me in his arms and absorbed my tears so many times. And we've always shared the dream of a bright future, and seeing those monarchs. If he leaves forever, there will be a big hole in my life.

He sighs deeply. "I was so afraid..." His hand sweeps through the air, the gesture vaguely indicating the living room and kitchen, everything around us. The light from the nearby lamp reflects in the tears filling his eyes.

I'm not sure when Emilio came to the United States, but he was a senior in high school when I moved into his household. He and I and his aunt Marisela and her twins moved from one temporary house to the next, picking crops throughout the Pacific Northwest. I lived with the family for nearly three years after Marisela found me on the street.

Marisela now has a steady year-round position as the caretaker for a big orchard, and although the house she and Kai and Kiki share is a perk of the job, the place is barely big enough for three. My house at WildRun is the closest thing Emilio has to a home where his family can gather.

"You'll always be welcome here, Shadow," I promise.

I glance at Sabrina, who nods again. "Of course."

"And Lilia, too," I add. "I can't wait to meet her." Did I already say that?

"*Gracias*, Tana." He hugs me for real this time, and then he embraces my housemate. "Thank you, Sabrina."

Later, when I lay my head on my pillow, I try to sort out why Emilio's revelation has bruised my soul so painfully. I didn't really want to marry him, after all. But Emilio Santos has always been there, like Marisela, holding me up, wishing me well, teaching me how to survive poverty, American-style.

Now he's moving on, leaving me behind. Now I will be no more than his kid sister.

It will be Lilia who gets to see the monarchs.

The next morning, when I see Emilio's blankets folded neatly on the couch and notice the flattened grass where his rental car was parked, my heart aches all over again.

All day long at the zoo, as I change the bedding for the big cats and wolves and bears in the cement caves that pass for their dens, I tell myself how irrational this injured feeling is, because I was never really his fiancée. He may have told the military that, but he never asked me. Everyone just presumed Emilio and I would end up together.

Which somehow makes it hurt even more.

At least Emilio's new love life and my depressing thoughts about my lack of same provide me with some distraction. For a few days, I think about something other than the murderous QTL scheme and my constant worry over what's happening to Penny and Grand and Marianne and all those innocent people around the world.

But then I get a text from Penny saying that she pulled it

off, she swapped another batch of Ebola-laden cosmetics, and she has photos and a lab report to prove it.

We're good to go, she texts.

I stare at that message for a long time.

Go where?

And do what?

Thirty-Three

It rains all the next day as I clean the poop-monster monkey cages at the zoo. What's worse than cleaning up crap? Cleaning up crap in the rain. So I'm glad that most of the monkey habitat is indoors, and I can shut them outside while I clean the interior sections and dry out a bit. As I shovel and scrub and hose down the cages, I try to come up with a resolution to my current dilemma. Nothing comes to me. At least no way I can think of to convince the right people about what Quarrel Tayson is up to. When the former president of the United States threatens you, who is safe to talk to?

Sabrina has been great since I got home. She loans me her truck when I have to work and she doesn't, which is frequently, since I'm working seven days a week to pay back the others who filled in for me while I was gone. It's my turn to cook tonight, so I stop to get the makings for hamburgers and sweet potato fries after I pick up Aaron at his private school. When we drive up to our house, I see someone waiting in the shadows on our front porch. I can't see the face clearly, but I can tell it's not Sabrina. Not Marisela, either.

It makes me nervous when people I don't know come to WildRun; that's why we have an electronic gate with a camera. This is my safe place. Bailey's sanctuary.

Did my housemate let a friend in? Sabrina knows people from her past that I've never met, and some of them are criminals.

"Who's that?" Aaron asks as he jumps out of the passenger side, his feet squishing on the wet ground.

I open my door, grab my sack of groceries, and slide out into the rain to follow him. In the distance, I see Bailey ambling out of the woods to greet us, the goats Salt and Pepper trotting behind him, always hopeful we'll have something edible in our pockets to share.

When the visitor steps out of the porch shadows into the gloomy daylight, my mouth goes dry. My body turns to ice. I put out a hand to stop my brother. It's a woman, wearing camouflage pants and a matching shirt.

I've seen her before in Bellingham, but then she wore a skirt and turtleneck. Now she's dressed like a hunter.

Maxine Newsome.

Mom's old colleague at QTL, the one who called my family vermin and said my parents deserved what they got.

Ignoring the rain that's wetting her hair and clothes, she calmly crosses her arms. In one hand, she holds a humongous hunting knife. "I suspected it was you," she says to me. "How *could* you?"

I visited her house in Bellingham last year, pretending to be a college student. Has she really known since then that I was

Amelia Robinson? "I don't know what you're talking about."

I thought she was an old lady, but now I realize that if she was a colleague of Mom's, she's probably not yet fifty.

What is she doing here? Why is she wearing camo? Why is she carrying a knife?

I'm trembling with fear. I hear a pounding sound high overhead, or more likely, *in* my head. "How did you get in here?"

"And you." She levels the knife at Aaron, and now I see that it's dripping blood mixed with rain water. "I didn't have to save you. All those years, I paid to protect you."

My brother is frozen in place, rain running down his cheeks, his eyes fixed on the bloody knife, his mouth half open.

She turns to me again. "And you *still* can't leave it alone?"

"I don't know what you're talking about," I repeat. My voice sounds like a small child's, high and squeaky.

The paper grocery sack I'm clutching is getting soggy and may not hold up much longer, but that seems like a pretty irrelevant thought to be having right now.

"I saw the photo." She narrows her eyes and swipes drips away from her forehead. "Zimbabwe. Taking property that wasn't yours."

How did she get that photo? Elaine? Garrison?

Is that blood behind her on the front steps?

My hair is dripping into my eyes, but I'm afraid to even raise a hand to push it out of my face. Oh God, where is Sabrina? Will I find my housemate's body on the dining room floor in a pool of blood like Mom and Dad?

Beside me, Aaron makes a strangled sound. Then he

whispers, "She's a ninja."

I glance at him. "What?"

His eyes are huge. His clothes are wet, sticking to his thin torso, and every muscle in his body is clenched. "Her neck! Look at her neck! She's a ninja!"

I feel Aaron's hysteria rising. I'm desperately trying to control my own.

When I saw her at her house in Bellingham, a turtleneck covered the tattoos I can clearly see now on the left side of her neck. Three flying birds rise out of the collar of her shirt. That's the ink I saw between turtleneck and ski mask on a murderer's neck the night my parents died.

My parents died surrounded by pools of blood, most likely from knife wounds.

All these years, I assumed the killer was a man.

"Run, Amelia, run!" Aaron shrieks.

Thirty-Four

My brother races away toward the trees, splashing through puddles and flashing past Bailey, who skids to a stop. He waves his trunk in the air, confused now about which way to go, which human to protect.

Does Maxine have a gun stuck in the back waistband of her pants? I watch her carefully to make sure she doesn't shoot my brother or my elephant. But she squints her eyes again and shakes her head as Aaron vanishes into our woods.

I want to follow my brother, but what would happen then? Would she throw that knife? Pull out a gun and shoot me in the back? Or would she simply wait until we came out of hiding and kill both of us then? Does she have accomplices hiding in those woods? Is Aaron already a captive again?

"My husband killed himself because of your mother and father." Maxine pushes a hand through her wet hair, leaving furrows there. "He was weak that way; we were only doing what had to be done."

What had to be done?

Did this woman wield the knife that slit Mom and Dad's throats? Who made that decision to kill my family?

"I saved so many jobs. But your mother and father were so selfish." She grimaces. "I still lost my career. I've made too many sacrifices."

Sacrifices? I've been inside her beautiful house on a cliff with a view of Chuckanut Bay. How about Mom and Dad swimming in their own blood? How about Aaron's years of drugged imprisonment? How about me, homeless and on the run at fourteen?

"You need to be reasonable, girl," she tells me. "Forget about whatever you think you've discovered. Nobody else needs to get hurt. We can all live long, comfortable lives."

I know now exactly what the word *dumbfounded* means. My brain isn't working; my tongue can form no words. Rain drips off my nose. I'm rusting in place like the Tin Man in the Wizard of Oz. From the corner of my eye, I see Bailey start to move again in our direction. Maybe he'll stomp Maxine flat and end this standoff.

But she still has that knife.

As Maxine takes a step closer, the pulsing sound in my head grows louder.

Then that whop-whop-whop sound I've been hearing overhead reverberates downward, and a gush of air flattens what's left of our trampled garden. Like something out of a nightmare, a cliché black helicopter sets down just beyond the house, its whirling rotors ripping leaves from the trees and creating a cloud of mist.

Another camouflage-covered figure climbs out of the

helicopter, and, hunching over to avoid being decapitated, trots our way. Phineas Pederson, the mercenary. He has a pistol in his hand. He's the head of security at Quarrel Tayson Labs. The creep who took a photo of me at Maxine's house. The maniac who wanted to kill me with a kayak paddle. And most likely, the man who ordered all the drone invasions here at WildRun.

All my fears about QTL have come to life.

So it's not going to be an arranged accident for me after all, a speeding car propelling my bicycle into a tree or a hit-and-run in a mall parking lot. It's going to be a knife or a bullet that kills me in front of my house in the rain. I hope Pederson's aim is good, so it will be quick. I hope Aaron can stay hidden. I set my bag of groceries on the ground. The wet paper tears and the packages plop out into the mud at my feet.

Beyond the helicopter, Bailey dances on his back legs. His ears are extended, his trunk raised, because he wants to attack the mechanical beast, but he's terrified of the whirling blades.

Run, Bailey, run. I try to telecommunicate that to him. I can't bear to see my elephant chopped to mincemeat during my last moments on earth.

I expect Pederson to shoot me, but instead, he stops a few feet away. After scrutinizing me from head to foot, and he looks toward Maxine and calmly inquires, "You okay?"

"It's done." She wipes the knife on her pants, leaving a bloody trail across her thigh.

Oh God, what's done? Whose blood is that?

"We need to go." He twists his head back to me, his dark eyes blazing. He points the gun at my chest, and I expect the flash and the bullet at any second.

"You're just a kid," he growls. "But I know you understand what could happen here." He tilts his head toward the helicopter. "C'mon, Newsome."

Maxine dashes toward the helicopter, her boots squishing in the wet grass.

Pederson's gaze is cold and inscrutable, like a reptile's. "Your future is completely up to you, Amelia. There's nobody to tell, and even if you did, nobody's going to believe you. All you and your friends have to do is keep your mouths shut." He starts to turn away, then stops and says over his shoulder, "You know what will happen if you don't."

He returns to the helicopter, backing the last few steps as he points his gun at Bailey, who is frantically hopping from foot to foot, ears out, trunk in the air. For a long moment, I'm afraid Pederson is going to shoot my elephant. But he climbs into the chopper seat behind the pilot. As the machine lifts off, a rock flies into a window of the helicopter. Cracks radiate out from the impact.

Aaron.

The helicopter stops ascending and hovers. My breath catches in my throat and my stomach does a back flip. If my brother is close enough to throw that rock, he's close enough to get shot. But he must be hidden, because after a few seconds, the chopper swiftly rises and vanishes into the clouds.

I collapse to the ground, shaking.

Bailey's trunk wraps around my shoulders and he bumps me gently with his forehead. He nudges the groceries with a foot, and steps on one corner of the package of hamburger buns, flattening a quarter of the contents. He's huffing, still frightened.

I'm so glad my elephant didn't walk into those blades. I wrap both arms around his trunk and kiss it, grateful that he's here with me.

The puddle I'm sitting in is soaking through my pants. I don't want to walk through my own front door, afraid of what I'll find. Because of that rock, I know that Aaron's probably okay, at least physically. But before my brother comes back to the house, I need to pull myself together and go in. If my housemate is dead on the floor, seeing her body might put Aaron back in the mental ward.

Gravel crunches behind me. I leap to my feet, expecting another attack.

Sabrina rides up on my bike, clad in her waterproof jacket and rain pants. Pulling my helmet off her head, she looks at me quizzically. "What's going on? Why were you sitting out here? It's your turn to cook, you know."

Thirty-Five

In the kitchen, we find one of the goats, its head nearly severed from its body. The elderly gray goat that someone dropped off at our gate only a few days ago. It was so arthritic that it was probably the easiest to catch. I grieve for its pointless murder, but thankfully the poor animal hasn't been at WildRun long enough for us to name it, let alone develop any real affection for it.

I have no choice but to tell Sabrina everything. She knows I started life as Amelia Robinson and that my parents were murdered. She's been with me through drone assaults and one previous household invasion, too. Her expression is tense but calm as she helps me mop up the blood and carry the poor goat's body out back for burial. I'm thankful when the rain finally lets up.

"I get it," Sabrina says. "They're showing how they could get us at any time."

As the child of a drug-addict mother with a lot of criminal connections, one of whom has vowed revenge on her for putting him in jail, Sabrina considers our pasts equal. That "us" tugs at my heart, and I tell her, "It's me they want."

But she's right; they'll target her, too. And Aaron. Who knows how far the bloodbath might extend?

Sabrina's wrong about our troubles being equal. There's really no comparison between our situations. My problems have escalated to a global scale. It's not a race I wanted to win.

After we've hidden the corpse and I've put on some clean clothes, I finally go to find my brother. He's sitting against a tree in the far corner of the property, and of course, Bailey is with him. Salt and Pepper are there, too, their shaggy coats wet and dirty. When Aaron lifts his tear-stained face to look at me, all I say is "They're gone."

He doesn't say a single word as we trudge back to the house, an elephant and two goats trailing us. I don't know how we're going to get to sleep tonight.

Maxine Newsome mentioned saving Aaron. I know that an M.C. Smith from White Rock, British Columbia, was listed as my brother's guardian when he was held captive in a special school as Jaime Ramirez. After asking Bash to arrange for some sleuthing through Canadian records, the two of us deduce that Maxine Newsome was Maxine Clementine Smith before her marriage to Carl Newsome, a QTL geneticist working in Bellingham. In the Social Security death index, Carl's date of death is listed six months after my parents were murdered. He must have been the other ninja I saw that night. I guess Maxine or her husband couldn't bring themselves to slaughter a nine-year-old boy. In her house, I saw a photo of her grandson, a little younger than Aaron.

Does that indicate that Maxine has a conscience? Somehow, I don't think so.

I'm still not clear what part Pederson played then, if any. But he's obviously a well paid thug who could efficiently and calmly get rid of anyone for the right price.

I've worked so hard to keep myself and my past as close to invisible as possible. But now I realize that the problem with staying off the radar is that it would be easy to erase a tiny blip like me without anyone noticing.

I can't let that happen.

And I can't let QTL continue with their crimes. How could any moral person turn a blind eye to the evidence and leave a serial killer at large?

I can think of only one way that I might be able to expose QTL and protect everyone in my life. But it's risky; it could also put them all in the enemy's crosshairs and get them all killed. And I need Aunt Penny's technical skills to pull it off.

"I've been hiding for over four years now," I tell her on the phone. "But they know enough about me to find me and everyone I touch. They could kill me at any time, and nobody would know why."

"I am aware, sweetheart," she says in a quiet voice.

Of course she is.

"I can think of only one way that might stop them." And then I tell her about how her past exploits inspired my plan.

"That's brilliant!" she responds. "I can be there within a week, and I can definitely assist."

"It will take me at least that long to assemble all the

photos I need and write the script."

"Get on it, Tana."

So I spend the next week with my cell phone in hand, taking photos of Aaron, Sabrina, Bailey, the cats, the goats, even all my colleagues at the zoo—any living acquaintance of mine who could be used as leverage against me. I already have good photos of Marisela, Kai, Kiki, and Emilio. And there are multiple shots of Bash on my phone, so I sort through those and pick one where The President's Son is looking right at the camera.

I even include Catie Cole and Jason and Xavier Jones, my favorite racing buddies, and my sponsors Clark and Kent Nilsen, hoping that they'll all forgive me afterwards. Penny supplies good close-ups of Grand and Marianne and herself. I have to cut Mom and Dad from their work photos to include them; it's sad that those are the only pictures I have of them.

I clip the photo of Maxine Newsome from those same work photos, and grab Phineas Pedersen's Chief of Security image from the Quarrel Tayson Laboratories website, and I even manage to find Elaine on their Overseas Executives page. Seeing those faces again makes me quake inside.

Finally, I download Liz Abbott's selfie from my phone to my computer. I wish I could apologize in advance to her parents.

All in all, I have thirty-nine photos to deal with. I put them in order for the slideshow I have in mind. And then I write my script. Just reading it aloud makes my heart palpitate.

How can I do this? How can I not?

Will I be able to survive the shit storm that will inevitably rain down afterwards?

Eight days later, Penny arrives. I can't let her come to the house yet, so we meet in secret at the local hotel where she's staying. We agree that I will introduce her to my family after the deed is done. Her cover will be blown then, anyway.

I don't sleep at all the night before; I spend most of the hours of darkness sitting under the stars with Bailey by my side. He knows something is up; he keeps wrapping his trunk around my shoulders and messing up my hair. I remember that matriarch elephant in Zimbabwe. She was so fierce she was in fighting for her comrades.

"I'm doing this for you, Bailey," I explain, caressing his trunk and then his ear. "And for everyone I love."

Although I'm a zombie from lack of sleep, I still have to go to work the next day. After I empty my wheelbarrow of manure into one of the zoo's compost heaps, I lean on my shovel and stare at the odiferous pile of crap for several minutes.

"What's up with you?" another Habitat Maintenance Technician in the compost yard asks. He's new; I think his name is Jared. Or maybe Garrett. The regular zookeepers have uniforms and nametags. We have stained coveralls.

I tilt my head toward the hill of dung I just added my barrow load to. "I'm thinking about crawling in."

He gives me a quizzical look. "Is that a joke? I don't get it."

"You will soon." I leave him standing there, pitchfork in hand, confusion twisting his features. I wonder if he'll be here tomorrow.

I wonder if *I'll* be here tomorrow.

Thirty-Six

Penny and I have agreed on nine minutes after seven in the evening, West Coast time. People who watch television should have their sets on then, and it'll be between commercials, so they'll probably be in their chairs. And the internet junkies and everyone watching shows on other devices will likely be glued to their tablets or phones or laptops.

Penny said she'd do her best for both television and widespread internet coverage, which should get most of the streaming services, too. She warned me that our video won't appear everywhere, and the live feed may get cut off before the whole thing is shown. She's busy plastering the recording on sites everywhere right now, so people will be able to search for it for a while, anyway.

Seven comes, and I move the laptop from my bedroom to the living room, setting it down next to the television, where Sabrina is watching a show about building elaborate treehouses.

"What the hey?" She points at my laptop, which is

currently displaying a news site.

"You'll see."

The minutes tick down, my pulse rate increasing with each one.

Seven oh nine.

I may throw up.

Then the television screen changes simultaneously with the laptop screen. A loud buzzing burp like an electrical surge fills the airwaves, and a mechanical voice announces: "This is the Emergency Alert System."

On the kitchen countertop, my cell also announces this, even though I didn't answer any call. Wow. I haven't heard that notice for so long, I didn't even know the Emergency Alert System still existed. Obviously Aunt Penny knew.

Then my face fills all the screens, and I say, "Some of you know me as Tanzania Grey. But my real name is Amelia Robinson."

Sabrina gasps and leans forward.

"I've been living under a false identity because four years and eight months ago, Quarrel Tayson Corporation murdered my parents, Amy and Alex Robinson." Their pictures replace my face on the screen as my voice continues, "Quarrel Tayson is still murdering people today by spreading Ebola around the globe."

"That's right. They distribute new strains, and then they sell a new vaccine to prevent it. We have irrefutable proof." Penny gave me that word, irrefutable.

The television screen abruptly goes completely blank, but the computer screen continues to play the video. Aaron walks into the room and stops behind the couch, staring at the screen.

"My mother and father discovered their secret; that's why they were killed. The Quarrel Tayson thugs kidnapped, imprisoned, and tortured my brother Aaron for years. More recently, they killed one of their couriers, Elizabeth Abbott, after she accidentally contracted the Ebola strain she was transporting." The selfie hurts to view; Liz looks so happy.

"And now they threaten me and everyone I care about." All the photos I collected appear one after the other on the screen, overlaid with their printed names and with my voice identifying each person. My adopted family, my relatives in Zimbabwe, my co-workers at the zoo, my sponsors.

"I also have an elephant that I saved from slaughter, and other animals I love." Bailey's photo heads the parade of pictures of my four-legged companions at WildRun: three cats and six goats now.

"Quarrel Tayson may seek to murder any or all of these individuals and animals. Along with her husband, this woman, Maxine Newsome, murdered my parents four years ago. This man, Phineas Pederson, has protected Newsome and threatened me." I picture both Maxine and Pederson gasping in shock at seeing their photos on the screen. "This woman, Elaine Kuska, has distributed Ebola throughout Africa for Quarrel Tayson." *Take that, Elaine.*

"If I or any of my loved ones die, you'll know why. It's all about the money. Think about it: Planting and then eradicating new strains of Ebola provides a guaranteed constant revenue stream, doesn't it? Ask yourself: How many have benefited from that? How many knew what was going on? Then ask yourself: How many have died?"

The video ends. The computer display returns to the normal news articles. The television screen is still blank.

Aaron points at the computer. "Back it up. Back it up!"

"I can't. That was a temporary interruption, Aaron. But maybe..." I switch over to YouTube, and sure enough, there's my video, stacked at the top of the Trending list.

He grabs the laser mouse from my hand and drags the slider through the photos until he gets to Penny. *Penelope Anne Patterson Joubert*, the on-screen label reads.

"Mom!" His tone is halfway between a moan and a prayer. He turns to look at me. "It's Mom, isn't it?"

I put my hand on his arm and try to make my voice as gentle as I can. "Aaron, that's not Mom. That's Aunt Penny; I met her in Africa. Her whole name is Penelope Anne Patterson, just like it says. Turns out that Mom's real name was Piper—Piper Amy Patterson."

He vehemently shakes his head. "No, it's Mom."

He turns to stare at Penny's image on the computer screen. I know that kind of yearning. It's makes your whole body ache, and it hurts me to watch it in my little brother.

I wrap my arm around his shoulder. "I know you want Penny to be Mom. I did, too. Mom and Aunt Penny were identical twins; that's why they look so much alike."

He shoves me away, his eyes fierce. "Stop saying 'was'! It's Mom!"

"It's not, Aaron. And you're going to see for yourself, because Aunt Penny will be here in just a few minutes."

He pivots eagerly toward the front door.

Sabrina is still sitting on the couch, stunned, her eyes focused on a ticker at the bottom of the television screen: *Breaking news: Quarrel Tayson Corporation accused of mass murder...*

My cell phone is bleating; and then Sabrina's buzzes, too. She ignores hers; I pick up mine and answer without even checking caller ID.

"What the hell was *that?*"

Thirty-Seven

I t takes me a minute to identify the outraged male voice. "Shadow—"

"Don't you dare call me that, Amelia Robinson! You lied to us all these years. I don't even know who you really are."

"You know who I am, Shadow...Emilio. You just didn't know my birth name and my past history."

He hangs up.

Crap. Two more people call, Nathan Ransek from the zoo and fellow racer Xavier Jones, asking if that was real. I assure them it was.

Ransek says "Whoa! Deep!"

X responds "Cool!"

I promise to call X later to tell him about everything he missed in Zimbabwe, because now my phone is beeping for Call Waiting and the intercom is chiming, too, signaling that Penny's at our front gate. I buzz her in and then answer my incoming call as I follow Aaron outside onto the porch. Bailey's lumbering in our direction, having heard a car enter through the front gate.

"What the hell was *that*?" a male voice says into my ear.

Didn't I just hear those exact words? Not many people have my cell number, but still, it's going to be a long night. I pull the phone away from my ear to look at the name on the screen. Clark Nilsen, one of my sponsors from Dark Horse Networks.

"Clark?"

"Kent's here, too. Was that for real, Tana?"

"Yes. I'm sorry I couldn't ask your permission first, guys. I understand if you want to drop me—"

"Drop you? Are you insane? This is the sort of thing we live for. We're going to help you in every way we can."

Kent chimes in. "We'll splash that vid all over the dark net. They'll never be able to erase it. How did you break into the Emergency Alert System, anyway?"

"I didn't. You'll have to ask my Aunt Penny about that. She's driving up right now."

Penny slides out of the driver's seat and pandemonium erupts.

Bailey trumpets and pounds closer, his ears standing out rigidly in warning.

Aaron shouts, "Mom!" and throws himself into Penny's arms.

Bailey slams to a halt and explores this combo human with his trunk, flapping his ears and trumpeting, unsure how to attack the intruder without injuring the boy he wants to protect.

"Friend, Bailey!" I yell, "Friend!"

Sabrina's standing behind me on the porch, talking into her phone. "Yes. I knew. Most of it, anyway."

Aaron plasters himself to Penny like a starfish clinging to a rock. "Mom," he sobs, "Mom, Mom, Mom!"

I know exactly what he's going through. *Sorry*, I mouth to Penny.

Her eyes shiny with tears, she mouths back, *it's okay*. As I advised, she has pulled her hair back into a French braid, which makes her look a little less like Mom, but still, I know the warm river of hope that is surging through my brother's head right now, side by side with a chilling stream of disappointment that he's not yet ready to acknowledge.

Bending her head, Penny murmurs, "I'm your mom's sister, her twin, your aunt Penny. I'm so happy to meet you, Aaron." She strokes her fingers through his hair and down the back of his neck, but he still doesn't let go of her.

"Tana? Tanzania?" a tinny voice says from the area below my neck.

I'm holding my cell phone against my chest. I pull it back up to my ear. "Clark? You and Kent still there?"

"Did we hear elephants?"

"Only one. Here's my Aunt Penny. She can tell you about the video." Then a dark fear grabs me. "But wait, guys! You can't tell anyone who she is, because that stunt was illegal, wasn't it?"

One of them makes a scoffing noise.

Kent says, "Majorly."

Clark adds, "We'd never reveal her secrets. Or yours, Tana."

"Okay. She probably won't tell you, anyway." I hand my cell to Penny, saying, "My sponsors Kent and Clark Nilsen from Dark Horse Networks—you can trust them. If you want to. They say they'll help."

While she talks to them, I pull on Bailey's ear to guide him away before my aunt and brother are covered in elephant slime.

My elephant lowers his head and I rub his forehead wrinkles between his eyes. Bailey rumbles with pleasure, I feel him vibrating like a purring cat. The past few weeks have been hard on him, too.

This morning, Wordage served me *cathartic*, an adjective that means *creating a sense of intense emotional, spiritual, or psychological purification after an intense emotional experience*. That's how I feel right now: exhausted but cathartic.

For better or worse, my life is now changed forever.

I send Bailey off toward the barn and his goat friends, and when I return to the house, Sabrina has brought Penny and Aaron inside to the kitchen table. Penny has a glass of wine in front of her. Emilio must have left a bottle here. Aaron has apple cider. My brother can't take his eyes off Penny's face, but now he's asking her about Africa, so maybe he's adjusting. I pour myself a glass of wine, too, which makes Aaron's eyes widen. Then for good measure, I pour the last of the bottle into Sabrina's glass.

I've turned off the sounds on my cell, but the face of the phone keeps lighting up with texts. My colleagues at the zoo. Kai. Kiki. I ignore most, but I see that Kent Nilsen has asked

Can we be your agents?

I have no idea what he means by that. I have zero intention of writing a book, but I answer *Sure.*

In case of invading ninjas tonight, I give Penny my bedroom and prepare to sleep on the couch. Although I've tucked a baseball bat under the couch, I'm not naïve enough to think that I could really defend my household. But it seems only fair that I make the attempt and if necessary, that I am the first to die.

As I tuck in the sheets, Emilio's angry message echoes in my head. There's been no word from Marisela or Bash. Did they miss the broadcast, or are they furious, too?

Bash texts me the next morning: *Congratulations.*

I didn't tell him what I was going to do, so I'm not sure whether he's being sarcastic or sincere. I'm afraid to ask if he's getting an earful from Garrison.

Thirty-Eight

The week that follows the broadcast is insane. Sabrina, Bash, and I keep waiting to be murdered. Maybe Aaron too, although I don't suggest the possibility in case he hasn't thought of it yet.

Former President Garrison doesn't call me or Bash. Maybe he thought it was his patriotic duty to protect an enterprise as huge and vital to the economy as the Quarrel Tayson empire.

Maybe he knew what they were up to all along.

I suspect we'll never know the truth.

Dark Horse Networks is flooded with emails to me. I'm sure many are death threats, but they don't let me see those. I'm so grateful Clark and Kent have always been willing to be my firewall against the public, but I'm still overwhelmed by the messages they choose to share with me. Some people write about how they've always suspected the huge pharma corporations were up to no good, and some relate sad tales of loved ones dying because they couldn't afford a drug they needed. But most surprising, hundreds of people volunteer to protect me and my family and home.

I don't accept, of course, because I don't want so many strangers to know where I live, but still, it gives me the warm fuzzies to know all these folks support me.

A farm in eastern Washington volunteers to donate a truckload of hay for Bailey and the goats. I gratefully lower my guard enough to let that in.

I learn why the Nilsens volunteered to be my agents when several television shows invite me to be a guest. Kent and Clark sift out two that will treat me well, and negotiate a price for my appearance that I would never have dreamed of. I upchuck before each interview, but on camera I manage to make it through my story without puking by telling myself I have to do this now so I'll never have to do it again.

All the authorities deliver their standard noncommittal, uninformative speeches: "We're investigating the allegations." "We will prosecute if laws have been broken."

Through it all, there's absolutely no response from Quarrel Tayson Corporation.

Nada.

Do they think the scandal will just go away if they don't acknowledge it?

Or are they biding their time as they plot their revenge?

Thirty-Nine

Finally, after nearly three weeks, the CEO of Quarrel Tayson Corporation purchases a prime time slot on television. He appears behind a huge desk, his hands folded on top of its shining wood surface like he's giving a presidential talk from the Oval Office. Displayed prominently behind him is the plaque awarding QTC the Congressional Medal of Honor, as well as a bunch of other awards and certificates, and of course, a huge American flag.

Looking directly into the camera, he intones in a deep voice, "We owe a huge debt of gratitude to Amelia Robinson, also known as Tanzania Grey, for alerting us to a rogue operation at Quarrel Tayson Laboratories involving the deadly Ebola virus. The few employees involved in these unspeakable criminal acts have all been fired and will be held responsible for their crimes."

"Although the Quarrel Tayson Corporation had no knowledge of their activities, the Board wishes to extend our profound apologies to anyone adversely affected. We have established trusts for Amelia Robinson and Aaron Robinson, awarding each of these children two million dollars, which we know can never replace their parents, but will help to ease their futures."

A few days later, Quarrel Tayson Laboratories announces that thanks to their efforts, Ebola will soon be eradicated from the planet, and their gene-splicing wizards are well on their way to finalizing a vaccine to prevent Alzheimer's disease.

I choose to believe that is a real miracle that will help people. After all, my mother, Piper Amy Patterson Robinson *was* a real hero in the pharmaceutical industry.

And my dad, Alex Robinson, was a martyr for the truth.

Aaron and I videochat regularly with Penny, Grand, and Marianne. When Aaron is out of school this summer, we're planning on going on safari in Africa.

Marisela talks Emilio out of his snit and along with Kai and Kiki, and now Lilia, they will always be important members of my extended family.

The zoo decides I'm still fit to shovel manure, but now that I have money, I may cut down to part time because I want to go to college like Bash, and when he calls to congratulate me again, I ask him for advice about how to apply for admission.

I'd like to study something to do with wildlife conservation. I know the competition is tough to get into good schools and that with only a GED, I'm not exactly a prime candidate.

"Apply now while you're still the courageous whistleblower," he advises during a videochat. "I'm so proud of you, Tana."

He pauses to scratch his chin, which needs shaving, and then asks, "Or should I call you Amelia now?"

I tell him I'm thinking about that and I'll let him know when I decide.

"Fair enough," he says. "How's lover boy?"

"Who?"

He waits, staring calmly at me for the two seconds it takes for the answer to click into my brain. "You mean Emilio? He's still around, but we're not involved in that way any longer. He met someone else in California."

A very un-Bash-like storm of emotions flits over his face, and he lowers his gaze away from the screen. Then he takes a deep breath, swallows, and focuses his intense laser-green eyes directly on me again. "Choose me."

Like a bright light flashing into my eyes on a dark night, those words momentarily stun me. "What?" I whisper. "What about Mandy?"

He raises his eyebrows. "Who?"

That makes me smile.

He leans forward so his handsome face fills the screen. "Look, Tarzan. We know each other in ways nobody else ever will. I'm not ready to get married. Are you?"

"Oh heck, no, Bash."

"I'm not ready to give up racing. Are you?"

"No way. There are so many great courses left to run."

"There are. We both have important things to do."

"I like to think so," I tell him.

"But we need each other. We belong to each other. And we've nearly died together so many times."

Although it wouldn't be funny to most people, that last statement makes me laugh.

"So choose me."

"I will, Bash." My throat is threatening to close up, but I manage to croak out two more words. "I do."

Life is precious. So now, I choose to live it fearlessly and truthfully, and I choose to do that together with Sebastian Callendro. Although my past is an intricate weave of untruths, my whole life is not a tragic lie. It's an incredible story. Some parts are wonderful and some parts are horrific, but the story is unique and it's all mine.

I am proud to be now and forever more, Tanzania Grey.

If you enjoyed *Race for Justice*, please consider
writing a review on any online book site.
Reviews help authors sell books!
Thank you!

Acknowledgements

No writer can produce a good book alone. I owe a big THANK YOU to the following people, who read the drafts of this book and helped to improve the story: astute reader Jeanine Clifford, author Rae Ellen Lee (raeellenlee.com), and author Cherie O'Boyle (cherieoboyle.com). Thanks are owed also to author Sara Stamey (sarastamey.com) for her help in improving the book description.

Books by Pamela Beason

The *Run for Your Life* Young Adult Adventure Trilogy

RACE WITH DANGER
RACE TO TRUTH
RACE FOR JUSTICE

The Neema Mysteries

THE ONLY WITNESS
THE ONLY CLUE
THE ONLY ONE LEFT (Coming soon)

The Sam Westin Mysteries

ENDANGERED ✓
BEAR BAIT ✓
UNDERCURRENTS
BACKCOUNTRY

Romantic Suspense

SHAKEN
CALL OF THE JAGUAR (ebook only)

Nonfiction Ebooks

SO YOU WANT TO BE A PI?
SAVE YOUR MONEY, YOUR SANITY, AND OUR PLANET

Keep up with Pam by subscribing to her mailing list on
http://pamelabeason.com.

About the Author

Pamela Beason is the author of the Sam Westin Mysteries, the Neema Mysteries, and the Run for Your Life Young Adult Trilogy, as well as several romantic suspense and nonfiction books. She has received the Daphne du Maurier Award and two Chanticleer Book Reviews Grand Prizes for her writing, in addition to an award from Library Journal and other romance and mystery awards. Pam is a retired private investigator who lives in the Pacific Northwest, where she escapes into the wilderness to hike and kayak as often as she can.

http://pamelabeason.com

CPSIA information can be obtained
at www.ICGtesting.com
Printed in the USA
BVHW081102220919
559077BV00001BA/177/P